Grant was hit again by ✂ **P9-AFS-416**
her to him.

To kiss her again. To taste her one last time.

Instead he pulled her just an inch closer, stared into her eyes and whispered. "You're a Cain now. You can afford to stay anywhere you damn well want to."

She met his gaze head-on. It was different than it had been at the gala, when they were surrounded by people, when the lights were low and the music romantic. There, he'd almost believed she really was a Cain. Almost believed she wasn't the woman he'd once known.

But here, in this crummy motel, under the harsh cheap lights, here he couldn't ignore it. He couldn't pretend.

This was Meg. His Meg.

With her alabaster skin and her Cain-blue eyes.

She glared at him defiantly. "I am a Cain. I have always been a Cain. And this is where I want to stay."

His gaze dropped to her lips, and for a moment the urge to kiss her was almost overwhelming. Would she still taste like cinnamon and sugar? Would she still melt against him?

* * *

Secret Heiress, Secret Baby is part of the
At Cain's Command series: Three brothers
must find their illegitimate sister...or forfeit a fortune

Dear Reader,

I am much better at beginnings than I am at endings. Oh, I think I handle them okay, but they are always hard for me. Ends, no matter how good, are always a little sad and poignant. As a writer, they are doubly hard because I'm such a perfectionist and ending something means it's definitely completely done. There's no more time to wrap things up or finish things off.

This book is the end of the At Cain's Command series. It's the end of characters I have loved writing. This story has been so much fun to tell. These characters, with their deceptions and secrets, have been a joy to live with these past several years. I've adored them. I've hated some of them (Hollister, you know I'm talking to you!). There are even characters that I've hated in some books and liked in others. For me, that's the great thing about a series like this. We get to see characters change and grow. We get to see them through more than one set of eyes.

This whole series has been leading up to this book, Meg's story. It's the secrets surrounding her birth and life that drive the whole story. I hope you love these final pieces of the puzzle!

Emily McKay

SECRET HEIRESS, SECRET BABY

EMILY McKAY

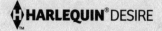

Recycling programs
for this product may
not exist in your area.

ISBN-13: 978-0-373-73388-0

Secret Heiress, Secret Baby

Printed in U.S.A.

HARLEQUIN®
™ www.Harlequin.com

Emily McKay has been reading romance novels since she was eleven years old. Her first Harlequin Romance book came free in a box of Hefty garbage bags. She has been reading and loving romance novels ever since. She lives in Texas with her geeky husband, her two kids and too many pets. Her debut novel, *Baby, Be Mine*, was a RITA® Award finalist for Best First Book and Best Short Contemporary. She was also a 2009 *RT Book Reviews* Career Achievement Award nominee for Series Romance. To learn more, visit her website, emilymckay.com.

Visit the Author Profile page at Harlequin.com or emilymckay.com for more titles!

For my dear son,
you may very well be the most charming man
I know, and I don't think I'm being partial either.

Prologue

After a mere three weeks of sleeping next to Meg Lathem, Grant Sheppard knew she was gone the instant he woke up. She liked to sleep curled against his side, one leg draped over his hips, her head resting on his shoulder. Of course, waking up at three or four in the morning only to find her puttering around the kitchen was normal.

He stumbled out of bed, pulled on the jeans he'd left draped over the rocking chair in the corner and went to find her.

In a house this size, it didn't take long. Her two-bedroom bungalow just a few blocks off the square in Victoria, Texas, was the house she'd grown up in. For a man like Grant, who'd grown up among the wealthy elite of Houston, this small town not far from the coast didn't hold much appeal. He had come here—and stayed here—for Meg.

She was baking again and the smell—a combination of toasted nuts and caramelized sugar—was divine.

That scent alone would have lured him out of bed.

He paused when he got to the kitchen, propping his shoulder against the doorway and watching her. Her inky-black Bettie Page hair was pulled up into a ponytail that bobbed enticingly as she moved. She'd thrown on a night-gown—something skimpy and sheer that hit her just below the curve of her butt. She'd put on an apron over that. Her feet were bare, her nails painted navy blue. The tattoo on the back of her leg peeked out from under the hem of her nightie when she bent over. She was sexier than a girl in a pinup calendar and every swish of her hem and wiggle of her ass made him ache with the need to claim her.

Between the retro kitchen and Meg's vintage style, he might have thought he'd traveled back in time to the forties. Only the blue nail polish and the tattoo ruined the illusion. That and the blowtorch she'd just lit up.

He knew better than to sneak up behind her while she was working. Instead, he just stood there and enjoyed the view, waiting as she skimmed the bright blue flame over the top of a pie's meringue, singeing the tips of the curlicues a golden brown. When she straightened and flicked the blowtorch off, he walked into the room.

"What'd you create this time?"

She shot a playful look over her shoulder. "I thought I heard you back there leering at me." Then she winked, cocking her hip slightly to show off her stupendous curves.

"And here I thought I was waiting patiently."

She turned around, her ponytail flicking over her shoulder. She held out a hand as if displaying the pie on the counter. "May I present my newest creation? Toasted-hazelnut graham cracker crust. Dark chocolate pudding. Toasted-marshmallow meringue topping. I'm calling it s'more pie."

He faked a groan of anguish. "And I have to wait until the shop opens to try it."

She grinned, stepping aside to reveal a second, tiny pie. "You know I'd never serve a pie at the shop that I hadn't tested. Just give me a second to toast the—"

But he didn't give her a second. He'd waited long enough. He strode across the room, slipped his hands under the hem of her nightgown to cup her—*hello!*—bare ass.

Her flesh was firm and warm in his hands and he only had to lift her a few inches off the ground for the apex of her thighs to graze against his throbbing erection. She arched, rubbing herself against him. Then he lifted her higher and she wrapped her legs around his waist. He backed her up half a step and let her ass rest on the counter behind her.

When he kissed her she tasted like sinful dark chocolate and meringue so sweet it was almost too much.

That was Meg all over. An irresistible combination of sinful and sweet. And always, almost too much.

Her hands found his zipper and eased it down, slipping into his jeans to free him. She wrapped nimble fingers around him and gave first one then a second long slow tug before she positioned him right between her lips. She rubbed herself against him, stroking the folds of her sensitive flesh first with the head of his penis and then—as she eased herself down his length—with her own fingers. She was desperate and needy and came almost before he did.

That was Meg all over. She was the sexiest woman he'd ever seen and she met him, passion for passion. She was almost too good to be true.

He wondered if she thought the same about him.

Later—a hot shower and a warm pie later—they were back in bed. She was almost drifting off to sleep as he traced the bared arc of her back, when he asked, "Why s'more pie?"

She sighed, nuzzled closer and muttered, "Because those are all the ingredients of s'mores, dummy."

"No. I meant what made you think of s'mores?"

She was quiet for a minute, and her breathing became so even and relaxed, he thought she'd probably fallen back asleep, when she said, "I don't know. Something about this—this thing between us—it feels like being at summer camp, don't you think?"

He chuckled. "Trust me. I did not do this at summer camp."

She gave his arm a swat. "No, silly. I mean it feels perfect but ephemeral. Like the last days of summer camp."

He sucked in a breath and held it, waiting to see what else she'd say. Because that was it, right there. The perfect moment. The moment he'd been angling for these past few weeks. *It doesn't have to be ephemeral. Come back to Houston with me. Marry me.*

It would have worked. She'd have fallen for it, just as she'd fallen for him.

But he didn't say it. He couldn't force the words out.

A moment later she said, "My grandpa used to make the best s'mores."

"I thought all s'mores were the same."

She seemed not to notice how stiff and formal he sounded.

"No, silly. The perfect s'more depends on the perfect toasted marshmallow. And Grandpa could roast 'em with the best. He was so patient." She was silent for several beats, and then added, "I wish you could have met him. You'd have loved him." And then came the kicker. "And he'd have loved you."

"I doubt that." He muttered the words, but she still heard them.

She pushed herself up on her elbow and looked down at him, her gaze still sleepy but firm. "No. He would have loved you. You're a good man, Grant Sheppard."

She pressed a kiss to his lips before settling back onto his shoulder.

An hour later, once she was deeply asleep, he got dressed and slipped out of her house. As he drove through Victoria for the last time, he could still taste her kisses and her pie on his lips.

Yeah, she believed he was a good guy. That had been

his plan all along: find Hollister Cain's missing daughter, make her fall in love with him, marry her and gain control of just enough of Cain Enterprises to drive the company into the ground.

It wasn't the plan of a nice guy. It was the plan of an asshole bent on personal revenge at any cost. Yeah, he could live with that. He was a bastard. He knew it.

The problem wasn't even that she didn't know it. The problem was, when she looked at him like that, he wanted her to be right. He wanted to be the man she thought he was. And that kind of weakness was completely unacceptable.

As he drove out of town, he started working on a new plan.

One

Just over two years later

Meg Lathem sat in her dusty, beat-up Chevy, cursing the blazing Texas sun, the crowded streets of downtown Houston and her tiny bladder.

She should have stopped at that Dairy Queen in Bay City to pee. Yes, she'd still be nervous as hell about seeing Grant Sheppard again after all this time, but at least she'd have a Dilly Bar to soothe the pain.

Instead, all she had was dry mouth and the beginning stages of an ulcer.

She chewed on her lip for a second. Then dug around in her purse for her lip balm. Instead, she found her cherry bomb lipstick, which she wore to finish up extra-long days when she needed a bit of sass and sex appeal to coast until the bakery closed. Today, she needed neither sass nor sex appeal. She needed sensibility and reason.

She shoved the lipstick back in her purse, slung the strap over her shoulder and was climbing from the car just as her phone rang.

If it had been any number other than her friend Janine's she would have let it roll over to voice mail. However, Janine—who usually helped manage the bakery—was watching Meg's daughter, Pearl, while Meg took this little jaunt to Houston, so she slid back into the car and shut out the noise of Houston traffic. She answered it with, "Is Pearl okay?"

"Pearl's fine, honey. She's happier than the cherry on a hot-fudge sundae."

The knot of anxiety in her chest loosened a smidge. "Then why are you calling?"

"You done it yet?"

"It's a two-hour drive from Victoria. No, I haven't done it yet. I just got here."

"Liar. You never met a speed limit sign you didn't love to mock. I bet you made it there thirty minutes ago and have been sitting outside his office making calf eyes at the words *Sheppard Bank and Trust* scrawled above the door."

"Am not." Meg glanced at her watch. She'd only been here for twenty-two minutes. And the words *Sheppard Bank and Trust* were not above the door. They were slapped on the outside of the building near the forty-second floor in ten-foot-tall letters. And she hadn't been making calf eyes at them so much as scowling. "I do not feel that way about Grant Sheppard anymore and you know it. That man is a lying, cheating sack of—"

"You don't have to do this," Janine said quietly.

"I know." She brought her hand up to her forehead and rubbed, pressing her thumb near the crest of her eye socket where the tension seemed to be drilling into her skull.

"We can find another way."

"I know," she said again. Except there was no other way. Her daughter needed heart surgery. Meg just couldn't afford to pay the insurance deductible and keep the bakery open. And if the bakery closed, then she'd be out of a job and really wouldn't be able to meet the deductible. The good people of Victoria had all banded together to do a fund-raiser for Pearl. The whole town had come together. It had been the most heartwarming, amazing day.

But they'd only raised nine thousand dollars. She needed almost fifty thousand for the surgery alone. Everyone she knew, everyone who loved and cared for Pearl, had banded together and dug as deep as they could. And it would only cover a fifth of the cost.

And even if she could somehow scrape together the money for this deductible, there was physical therapy. And more appointments down the road. And more specialists. More, more and more things to spend money on. Money she just didn't have. But Pearl's father had the money. Hell, money was his business.

Wasn't it only fair that he paid?

He was Pearl's *father*.

Going to him wasn't begging. It was only right.

But it would be so much easier if he already knew he had a daughter.

"Honey," Janine said, finally breaking the long silence. "Stop rubbing that spot above your eye. You know how sensitive your skin is and if you're going to see Grant Sheppard after all these years, you don't want to look all splotchy."

Meg jerked her hand away from her face and quickly flipped down the mirror. Crap. She did look all splotchy.

Then she snapped it closed. No, this was good. Splotchy was just fine. Humbling, even. A nice reminder that their relationship was never going to be sexual again. Never.

"Now, go get 'em, tiger. You can do this!"

Janine hung up then, not waiting for Meg to voice the doubts roiling in her gut.

"Right," Meg muttered. "Go get 'em."

She clambered out of the car and started crossing the street. Sheppard Bank and Trust opened up to a plaza with sprawling oaks, a trio of fountains and plenty of outdoor seating. The last of the lunch crowd was still enjoying the nice weather and even though Houston wasn't a town that got a lot of foot traffic, Meg had to weave around people as she reached the sidewalk.

She was still on the other side of the plaza when the big glass doors of the Sheppard Bank and Trust building opened and Grant Sheppard stepped out into the mid-afternoon sun. Her steps automatically slowed. A car honked somewhere, prompting her to dash the rest of the way across the street.

Suddenly she had tunnel vision. It was as if she could see only him and no one else. It had been over two years since she'd seen him. He looked good. Just as tall and fit as ever. His sandy hair was a little long. A little disheveled. A little renegade for this conservative town. But his suit was strictly business. It toed the line. His mouth still curled in that half smile. The smile that made a woman want to do naughty things to his lips.

The smile that made women stupid.

She gave her head a little shake and reminded herself—it wasn't just that it had been more than two years since she'd seen him, it was more than two years since he'd sneaked out of her bed in the middle of the night and disappeared without a trace.

Yeah, there was a difference, and she'd do well to remember it.

She hardened her heart and put a damper on her hormones before she took a step toward him. But as her tunnel vision eased up, she saw the woman standing beside him—a willowy blonde, almost as tall as he was. Even though she was thin, there was a softness to her body that was only emphasized by the protective hand he held at the woman's back. There was an intimacy to their posture that spoke of affection and familiarity. A warning bell went off in Meg's head.

She had stopped in her tracks, almost unaware of the other people filtering past her. She knew—even before the other woman turned around—what she was going to see. The woman would be beautiful and sophisticated and classy. Everything Meg was not.

She would also be pregnant.

Meg was so sure that when the woman actually turned so Meg could see her, Meg didn't comprehend what she was seeing.

Beauty—check. Sophisticated—check. But not pregnant. No. Worse.

The woman was holding a baby. A beautiful, healthy, bubbling baby. A "perfect" baby.

Grant Sheppard's beautiful socialite wife had given him a perfect, healthy baby.

Whereas the daughter he shared with Meg had Down syndrome and an atrial septal defect in her heart.

Meg never, ever thought of Pearl as being lesser. Yes, the tiny hole in her heart meant she had health problems that sometimes terrified Meg. But Pearl was perfect in her own way.

But would Grant see that? Would he realize how amazing Pearl was? Would she be able to protect Pearl if he didn't?

And beneath her basic mother's need to protect her child lingered some other, more complicated emotion.

Just the slightest twinge of envy that had nothing to do with the baby or with Pearl, but with the woman who appeared to be Grant's wife.

Meg didn't want to be that perfect blonde woman. She didn't want her wealth or her hair or her wardrobe or her baby—whose heart probably didn't have a hole in it. She loved her own bank account, hair, clothes and baby. She didn't want anything that other woman had. But for the first

time, she realized that part of her *might* still want Grant.
And that scared the piss out of her.

How could she go talk to Grant now?

The answer was, she couldn't. Not while she still had
any other options.

Instead, she would do the one thing she'd promised herself she'd never do. The thing she'd promised her mother
and her grandfather she'd never do. She'd go see her father.
She'd make a deal with the devil himself.

As luck would have it, the devil himself—aka Hollister Cain—lived a short drive from downtown in the prestigious River Oaks neighborhood. Nestled in among the
homes of former presidents, deposed foreign princes and
excessive country-music stars was her father's massive
antebellum mansion.

Thanks to Google Maps Street View, she knew the mansion by sight even though she'd never been there. For that
matter, thanks to Google Images she knew her father by
sight, too. She had never met him either.

No, she was Hollister's illegitimate daughter. Twenty-
six-odd years ago, he had seduced—and then abandoned—
her mother, not only because he was a heartless bastard,
but for calculated professional gain. Hollister's treatment
had led to her mother's slow but steady emotional unrav-
eling.

As a result, Meg had been raised by her grandfather.
All her life, she'd known the truth about Hollister and her
mother, so she'd naturally assumed that Hollister knew
about her too and had just never bothered to claim his
daughter. Which was fine by her. Just fine.

She certainly didn't need them or their money or the
misery it would bring to her life.

Except now she did need it.

Of course, there was a chance Hollister would flat out

refuse to acknowledge her. After all, Hollister was too much of a bastard to open his wallet willingly. Then lawyers would have to get involved. There would be genetic testing and all kinds of nastiness. But in the end, she was Hollister's daughter and there was nothing he could do about it.

But she didn't think it would come to that, because she knew secrets about Hollister's past that he wouldn't want getting out. She had proof of illegal things he'd done that would destroy the Cain family name. In his dealings with her family, he'd broken the law, and she had no problem letting him be judged in the court of public opinion. If he proved difficult, she would make whatever threats she needed to make.

So in her fairy-tale version, her reunion with her father would go down like this: she'd walk in, she'd announce who she was, he'd write her a check for a couple hundred grand, she'd sign some papers promising never to ask for more and she'd be back home with Pearl by the end of the week. What could be simpler than a little blackmail among family?

Still, she wasn't used to making threats like this. And two hundred thousand dollars was a lot of money. That was the number she'd ultimately decided she needed. Fifty grand to cover the surgery and another three times that much to cover anything else Pearl needed in the future. It was an arbitrary number and—hopefully—a little high. But this was a one-time thing. She had no intention of ever coming to Hollister for money again. This was her one chance to take the money and run.

Which probably explained the knots in her tummy as she stared out her grimy car windshield at the mansion across the street. Surely it had nothing to do with the memory, still so fresh in her mind, of Grant's hand low on the waist of that lovely blonde goddess.

Her phone buzzed and vibrated on the passenger seat. She ignored it as she climbed from the car. Janine had been calling her approximately every fifteen minutes for the past hour. No doubt wanting an update on how her "meeting" with Grant had gone. Meg didn't have the heart to tell her she'd chickened out. She would call Janine after she'd talked to her father.

She marched across the street and up the seemingly endless path, across a veritable sea of lush Saint Augustine grass, to the front porch. Before she could second-guess herself, she punched the doorbell. And then counted every second as it ticked by.

No one on the other side of that door mattered to her. Not at all.

Still, she'd been on her own a long time. And she was about to meet someone from her family. Maybe even her *father*.

Or maybe just someone who worked for her family.

Did the Cains have…servants?

Would there be a butler or something?

Or would—?

Then the door was opening and instead of her father, or even a servant, Meg was faced with a blonde woman with near-perfect features, a willowy athletic body and a faint bump at her belly. Portia Calahan. Dalton Cain's ex-wife. So, Meg's own ex-sister-in-law.

Meg would have recognized any of the Cains—thanks to their prominent position in Houston society and Google—but Portia she had actually met the first time she'd come to Houston, right after she'd learned Pearl would need surgery. She'd considered asking for financial help and then dismissed the idea just as quickly. She'd thought she'd slipped under everyone's radar.

For a moment, they just stared at one another. Then

Meg said, "What are you doing here?" at the same time Portia said, "It's you!"

Portia seemed to sway on her feet and her eyes rolled back. Her legs went out from under her. Meg lurched forward, dropping her purse, and caught Portia just as she crumpled to the ground.

Though Portia was thin, she was a lot taller than Meg. Meg, too, collapsed under Portia's weight and they both went down.

"Help!" Meg tried to control their fall, but she simply couldn't support Portia's weight. All she could do was try to lower Portia slowly as she muttered, "Shit, shit, shit, shit."

Not just because Portia had fainted, nearly hurting herself and crushing Meg, but because Portia was not supposed to be here! Portia wasn't part of the Cain family anymore. And Portia had obviously remembered meeting her.

For a moment, Meg considered bolting, trying to contact her father another day. Trying to get the money some other way. But she was out of time and she had no other way to get the money. And already footsteps were pounding across the tile floor toward them.

She looked up to see five more people crossing the foyer: two women and three men.

The men she all recognized. Her brothers. Dalton and Griffin Cain and Cooper Larson. If she had to guess, she'd say the two women were Laney and Sydney, her sisters-in-law.

To Meg's surprise, it was Cooper who quickened his pace and crouched down beside Portia. He gently cradled her head and shoulders, and Meg wiggled out from underneath her.

"She fainted," she said quickly. "I tried to catch her."

"Thanks," Cooper said, before muttering a curse under his breath. "She's going to be pissed."

"I tried to catch her!" Meg insisted again, scrambling back.

"Not at you," he said gently. "About fainting. It's the second time this week. She hates when it happens."

The red-haired woman—Sydney, if Meg remembered correctly from the pictures she'd seen in the society column of the *Houston Chronicle*—knelt beside Cooper and rested her hand on his arm. "Is she going to be okay?"

He nodded, but his smile didn't hide his concern. "The doctor says it happens to a lot of women in the first trimester."

Sydney looked up at Meg. "Thanks for catching— oh my gosh."

"Wait. What?" Meg asked, scooting farther away. Her gaze darted from Sydney to Cooper and then to the three people still standing. "I didn't—"

But when her gaze met Dalton's, he muttered a low "damn."

Now they were all staring at her. As in, she'd-grown-an-extra-head-or-two staring at her. Or, they-somehow-knew-she-was-here-to-blackmail-their-father staring at her.

Meg automatically got to her feet and held out her hands, palms out. "I haven't done anything wrong." Yet.

The other woman, Laney—who had long dark hair and resembled a modern-day Snow White—sent a chiding look at the others. "For goodness' sake, you're scaring her." Then she stepped forward, smiling. "No one thinks you did anything to hurt Portia. We're glad you were here to catch her. Aren't we?" She gave Dalton's elbow a little nudge.

He stepped forward too. "Yes, absolutely."

Meg looked warily from one sibling to the next. Gratitude for stopping Portia's fall did not explain their behavior. Panic edged in under her confusion. She took a step back toward the door. "You know, I think I'm going to go."

As one, Dalton, Laney, Griffin and Sydney took steps toward her as a chorus of protests echoed through the room.

Okay. This was getting weird.

She took a few more steps back toward the door. "I… um…"

"You can't leave," pleaded Laney. The rest of them stopped still in their tracks, as if Meg was some sort of spooked deer.

Great. She couldn't leave. She had unwittingly made some rich pregnant woman faint and now they were trying to keep her contained so they could call the police or something. Okay, that was probably a bit paranoid.

Portia must have been slowly coming to, because she made a groaning noise and pushed herself up onto her elbows.

"Why can't I leave?" Meg asked hesitantly.

"Not again." Portia looked around the room, blinking. "Did I miss anything?"

Cooper cradled her shoulders, gently brushing her hair out of her eyes. "You weren't out that long."

Laney took advantage of the distraction by stepping forward to clutch Meg's hand. "You can't leave because you're Hollister's missing daughter. You're their sister!"

"I know I'm their sister. How do they know it?"

Again, everyone turned to look at her and said, "*You* know?"

Two

Thirty minutes later—after Meg had nearly fainted, herself—the Cains finally lured her from the foyer into an elegant office in one of the front rooms. Dalton had poured drinks all around. Everyone else he knew well enough that he hadn't needed to ask what they wanted, but when he got to her, he shot her a look, his eyebrows raised in silent question.

"Just water, please." She needed to keep her wits about her. If there was one thing her mother had taught her, it was that rich people were all venomous snakes and the Cains were the worst. Like coral snakes. More deadly than rattlesnakes and twice as aggressive.

Once Dalton handed her the glass of water, he gestured toward a wingback chair, but she didn't sit down. Portia and Sydney were seated on the sofa opposite the chair. Laney was in another wingback chair beside it with Dalton standing behind her. The other two men were scattered around the room. The last thing she wanted was to be sitting in the hot spot.

"Okay, tell me again why you think I'm your sister."

Again it was Portia who answered. "Your eyes, obviously."

"My eyes?"

"You have the Cain blue eyes." Griffin pointed to one of his own eyes. Then he winked at her. "Very unique. All the Cains have them."

"You assume I'm your sister just because my eyes are blue? That's the stupidest thing I've ever heard! There have to be millions of people with blue eyes."

"Something like five million people have blue eyes, actually." Everyone turned to look at Portia. She shrugged. "I looked it up. The point is, eyes your exact color are unique."

"But not a reason to assume I'm a Cain."

Dalton leaned over to brace his elbows on the back of his wife's chair. "But you are, in fact, a Cain. Aren't you?"

She looked down at her glass of water and gave it a jiggle to move the ice around. "What if I am?"

"Then we've been looking for you."

"And," Portia added, "I think you've been poking around getting information about us, too."

For a second, Portia held Meg's gaze, before Meg looked back down at her water. Portia was right, of course. When she'd been in Houston a year ago, Meg had just wanted to get a feel for the Cains. She'd needed to gauge just how desperate she'd need to be before she went to them for money. She had even met Portia—introduced herself using a fake name, of course—and had a conversation with her. She'd been so sure that Portia hadn't suspected anything!

She forced her gaze back up to Portia's. She didn't say anything—didn't reveal that they'd met before—but there was a light of triumph in the other woman's gaze.

After several moments of silence, Laney and Sydney exchanged a worried look. Then Sydney spoke up. "Do you know why we've been looking for you?"

"No." All her life, she'd been told that her father had abandoned her and her mother and that no one in the Cain family wanted them. She couldn't imagine how they could have been looking for her when she lived in the same town where she'd been born, less than five miles from the courthouse where Hollister had married her mother. "There's no reason for anyone to be looking for me. I haven't exactly been hiding."

There was another tense moment as the Cains all looked at one another as if they were trying to decide who would be the best one to break the bad news to her.

Laney leaned forward. Okay, Snow White it was.

"I don't know if you know this, but Hollister's health has been declining for the past several years."

"If he recently died, don't feel like you have to break it to me gently." The father she'd never even met dying mere days before she finally decided to contact him? Yeah. That sounded about right. Not that she minded not meeting him, but it seemed unlikely that anyone else would care about her blackmail demands.

"Oh, no, Hollister is still alive," Laney reassured her. "But a few years ago, when he was at his worst and we were all sure he was going to pass, he received a letter." Laney paused and the Cains exchanged more awkward glances before Dalton gave her shoulder a little squeeze. "The letter was sent anonymously from a woman claiming to be your mother. She explained that she had born him a daughter many years ago and that she had purposely kept it from him to protect the girl. To protect you. But that she wanted him to go to his grave knowing that he could never get his hands on you. She was taunting him."

Meg frowned. "My mother couldn't have sent that letter. She died when I was a child." Plenty of people in her life hated Hollister, but none hated him enough to track his health obsessively just to drop that bombshell when he was on his deathbed. "I don't know anyone who would have done that. You don't think I did it, do you? Because—"

"No," Dalton said quickly. "We're not worried about

that. The woman who wrote the letter knew Hollister well enough to know it would drive him crazy—the fact that he had a daughter who was forever beyond his reach. So he set a challenge for the three of us." Dalton gestured to indicate his brothers. "Whichever one of us found you and brought you back into the fold would get his entire estate. If no one found you before he died, everything would go to the state."

"Excuse me?" For a long moment, that was all she could say. She couldn't even think clearly enough to process what he'd said, let alone to comment. Hollister was worth…well, she didn't know the precise numbers, but it was a buttload of money. Hundreds of millions at least. Finally she said, "What kind of—" she barely restrained herself from using the word *asshole* "—man sets up a crazy landgrab like that among his sons?"

Dalton just nodded. Griffin smiled grimly.

Cooper actually chuckled. "Yeah, exactly. Way to encourage sibling bonding, right?"

Except when she looked around the room, they *did* seem to be close. There wasn't even a glimmer of animosity among them.

"You seem to be getting along awfully well when there's so much money at stake."

Griffin shrugged. "We decided early on it was better to share information and split the money. Four ways, obviously. Besides, you've been pretty hard to find, given that we had zero information to go on."

"Except now that you've come to us—" Griffin looked around the room "—I guess we need to come up with a new plan. Should we give her the bigger share?"

"Wait, what? Her who? Her me?"

Laney smiled. "Obviously they were always planning on giving a quarter of the estate to you."

Panic shot through her and Meg lurched to her feet.

Even though she didn't know exactly how many hundreds of millions Hollister was worth, it was a lot. Any way she looked at it, a quarter of a lot of millions was a lot of millions.

She held up her hands, palms out, and started backing toward the door. "I don't want any of Hollister's money." Okay. That wasn't true. "I only want a tiny bit of money."

Laney stood up too and pulled out the Snow-White-coaxing-the-forest-creatures voice. "You seem upset by this news. Maybe you should sit down."

Sit down? Sitting down, with all the Cains staring at her, was the last thing she wanted to do. What she wanted to do was bolt from the room, hop back into her sensible Chevy and get the hell out of Dodge.

But with panic racing through her veins, she suddenly felt as light-headed as Portia had looked right before she'd fainted. That thought alone was enough to get Meg back in her chair. She wasn't a fainter. She never had been. Not even when she'd been pregnant. Not even when she'd been pregnant and working twelve-hour days at the bakery.

Nope. Not her.

She was tough. She wasn't a skittish purebred like Portia. She was strictly blue-collar, working stock.

She was not meant to be rich.

Rich people were assholes. Everything in her upbringing and her life had taught her that.

As her thoughts raced, she drew breath after breath into her lungs, desperate to find a way out of this. She had come here expecting to do a little light blackmailing and that… well, that was disconcerting enough. She hadn't expected things to get so out of control so quickly.

And then she slowly became aware that at some point she'd sat down and was cradling her head in her hands. When she looked up, it was to see all six of the Cains staring at her in total surprise.

Yeah. Clearly, they weren't used to people who were afraid of money.

It was Sydney who spoke first. "You know that Hollister is your father. But you seem surprised that anyone else knows or believes that you're Hollister's. And you don't seem to want the inheritance that is rightfully yours."

"I don't!" she said quickly. Thanks to the helpful pages of the *Houston Chronicle*, she'd seen what their lives were like. She was smart enough to know that kind of money came with strings a mile long and as strong as Teflon-coated titanium. She didn't want any part of that.

"Then why did you come?"

"I came because I need money."

Dalton gave her an impatient look. "You do realize that the inheritance from Hollister is worth a lot of money, right?"

"I'm poor, I'm not an idiot." She stood and marched over to the windows, staring unseeingly at the pristinely manicured lawns. From the corner of her eye, she might have seen Griffin punch Dalton in the arm. "I don't want an inheritance from Hollister. And I don't need money in two years or five years or wherever Hollister dies and the estate goes through probate. I need money now."

"How much?" asked one of the guys—she didn't know their voices well enough to know which one.

She glanced over her shoulder to see who had asked, and was surprised to see all three of the men reaching for their wallets. As if they'd just whip out two hundred thousand dollars in small bills.

"About two hundred thousand." She automatically rattled off the number she'd settled on to cover all of Pearl's expenses.

"For what?" asked Dalton after only a brief moment of silence.

"That's something I'll discuss with Hollister. When the

time comes." This was getting her nowhere. "Now, if you could just tell me where I can find him…"

Griffin stepped forward. "He's not here now. He just left for Vail. But when you meet him for the first time, one of us should be with you."

"So you can claim you found me and secure your inheritance?" she asked archly. Why the hell couldn't she have come to Houston on a day when Hollister was at home? It would have been so much easier dealing with one greedy bastard instead of six.

"Actually," Sydney said, "I think Griffin was offering more to protect you."

"I don't need protection from a dying seventy-year-old man." At least, she assumed she didn't. She was picturing Hollister as fairly weak, since they'd just described him as being on his deathbed. On the other hand, she was planning on blackmailing him. Which would probably piss him off.

"My father—" Griffin paused to gesture to her. "Our father isn't a very nice man."

"Yeah. I know that. I think I can handle anything he can dish out."

But again, before she could make it to the door, Dalton stopped her. "If you think Hollister is just going to hand over two hundred thousand dollars, you're wrong. He's going to make it as hard on you as possible. Because that's his MO."

Meg hesitated. Dalton could well be right. And she was prepared for that. She had never expected this to be easy.

She must not have had a very good poker face, because apparently her nerves showed in her expression.

"Why do you need the money?" Dalton asked.

She stiffened. "That's none of your business."

"Are you in trouble? Is it for something illegal?"

"No!" Indignant, she leapt to her feet.

"Look, I didn't mean to offend you," Dalton said. "I want to help."

Her gut reaction was eye-rolling suspicion and she didn't bother to hide it. "Right. Because the Cains are known for their altruism."

"Okay," he admitted with a wry smile. "I think we can work something out that will help both of us. If you can stick around for a few days, do things our way, get Hollister to acknowledge you and change his will, then I can get you the two hundred thousand dollars. Free and clear, on top of whatever you inherit from Hollister when the time comes."

Two hundred grand? The Cains must really be worried about losing control of that stock.

"And you can just come up with two hundred thousand dollars?" she asked, mostly to buy herself time to think.

Dalton shrugged. "Give me seventy-two hours and I can give you a hundred thousand in cash."

"Same here," Griffin said.

"Yeah, sure," Cooper added.

"So there you have it. You agree to stay long enough to prove to Hollister that you are, in fact, the daughter he's been looking for and you can have the money in three days. But you stick around after you get the money. You stay until we have a new will that no one can contest. Deal?" Dalton held out his hand.

She just stood there, staring at it. A handshake was still legally binding in Texas, after all. She had to be sure.

"If Hollister has been looking for me, why are you so worried about him believing I'm his daughter?"

They all looked at Dalton again, as if they were trying to decide how much to say.

Finally Dalton sighed, ducking his head slightly as he spoke. "Hollister's behavior has been erratic the last few years. The fact that he set up this challenge proves that. We'll all feel a lot better when his will is nailed down."

Okay, so they were worried about their own skins. At least that was a motive she could believe and understand.

A guaranteed two hundred thousand dollars sounded a lot better than facing Hollister with blackmail demands and hoping she didn't blink first.

On the flip side, it meant staying in Houston. At least three days. Maybe longer.

Janine, she knew, would be happy taking care of Pearl. But God...several days away from Pearl? On the other hand, it was a few days and it was only a two-hour drive. So she could make it back to Victoria if something serious came up.

She just needed to avoid Grant while she was in Houston. But how hard could that be? Houston was a city of more than two million people. All she had to do was lay low and stay out of his way while this was going on. Easy as pie, right? And she made pies for a living.

She held out her hand to Dalton. She'd come here expecting to make a deal with the devil and instead she was making one with the devil's son.

"Deal," she agreed.

This was so not her idea of laying low.

Meg stood in the doorway of the Kimball Hotel's grand ballroom, staring out at the two hundred or so people who made up the glitterati of Houston society. The Children's Hope Foundation's annual fund-raiser was one of the premier social events in the city. The average net worth in this room probably exceeded the GDP of most developing nations. Of course, she was there to bring down the average. Or at least, she would be if she could bring herself to step into the room.

At her side, Sydney gave her elbow a squeeze. "You got this. Come on, into the lion's den."

"Aren't they going to announce me or something?"

"I think they only do that in England."

"Okay." Meg blew out a breath, rubbed her palms down her borrowed dress, took one wobbly step forward in her borrowed heels and then abruptly stopped and turned around. Sydney and Griffin closed ranks on either side of her and turned her back around. "This is a horrible idea!" she protested.

"It's a fantastic idea!" Sydney muttered as she and Griffin steered her into the room. "Portia and Caro have been cochairing this event for years. It's their party. So when Portia introduces you as Hollister's long-lost daughter, no one will argue with her. When Caro welcomes you with open arms, it will seal the deal."

"Wait," Meg said. "Am I supposed to know who Caro is?"

"She's Hollister's ex-wife," Portia explained. "They divorced over a year ago. Things have been rocky for her, because Hollister tried to destroy her in the divorce, but she's back on her feet again and holds a lot of sway in this town."

Griffin added, "By the time Hollister gets back into town from his trip to Vail, the results of the genetic testing we did yesterday will be back from the lab. We'll have proof that you are our sister. Hollister will have to accept the results. You'll have the money from us by Monday."

"Right. By Monday. What could go wrong?"

For starters, she could trip and fall or generally make an idiot of herself. But that, that would just be small potatoes. No, her deepest fear involved running into Grant Sheppard.

That would be a total disaster.

She had tried to get Portia to show her the guest list—back when Portia had first proposed this plan—but Portia had dismissed her concerns, declaring, "Don't freak yourself out about the guest list. Yes, there are a few big names. Some politicians, a couple of sports stars. But it's nothing to worry about. No one scary will be there. And we'll be by your side the whole time."

That had been Meg's mantra ever since. *No one scary. No one scary. No one scary.*

Of course, their definition of *scary* might differ from hers. Mostly because she hadn't yet worked up the courage to tell them she'd had an affair with their4 business rival.

But surely Grant wouldn't come to this event. Yes, it was big, but why on earth would he come to a ball that was always chaired by a Cain?

As one, Meg, Sydney and Griffin moved through the room. With Griffin always introducing her as a valued member of the family, combined with Sydney's easygoing manner, the evening began to take on a surreal quality. At some point someone handed her a glass of champagne. And then another.

A lot of strategy had gone into planning who would bring Meg to the party and when everyone would arrive. Portia, Cooper and Caro had arrived at the party hours before the event actually began. Dalton had argued that he should bring Meg because now that Hollister didn't get out into society often, Dalton was ostensibly the head of the family. Griffin had countered that the consensus in Houston society was that Dalton was a brilliant businessman, but as Griffin had teased, "A cold and heartless robot."

"Your point?" Dalton had asked with an icily arched brow.

"That I should bring her," Griffin had answered easily. "That way, she'll meet a lot of people before you and Laney even show up. That way, everyone will be watching. Everyone will be waiting to see what happens when you and Laney walk in. Since everyone knows you're a heartless bastard, when you greet her, smiling warmly, the sight of you displaying actual human emotion will convince everyone she must be our long-lost sister."

Meg had tried to protest that the plan was overelaborate. There were too many elements. Too many things that could go wrong. But no one seemed to listen to her. And what did she know, really? She knew cakes and pies. Sweets and coffees. She knew that if you had more than three flavor profiles, you overwhelmed the palate, but that didn't mean she knew jack about…this. She didn't even have a word in her vocabulary for these kinds of social machinations.

All she could do was smile politely, try to remember names and avoid talking about…well, everything. Chances were good everyone she met thought she was a little bit stupid. Which was fine. She could live with that. All she needed to do was get through the next few days without incident and without running into Grant.

Quite honestly, she never wanted to see him or his beautiful wife again. She was still too angry over how he'd treated her. Too indignant. Too hurt. And—admittedly— too vulnerable to him.

Around the time someone handed her a third glass of champagne, Dalton and Laney walked in. They navigated the crowded ballroom more easily than anyone else, almost as if the crowd was parting to let them through. Just as Portia had predicted, everyone was turning to watch. Right on cue, Portia and Caro also converged on Meg. A united front.

Even though she'd known these people only two days, even though she didn't fully trust them and probably never would, she felt weirdly comforted by their presence.

She had no illusions about the permanence of their affection, but for tonight, they had her back. Before all of Houston society, they'd rallied around her.

In this moment, it truly seemed as if all of Houston society was there and watching. Laney stepped forward and pulled her into a hug at the same moment that Dalton greeted Portia, hugging the woman who was his ex-wife and current sister-in-law with genuine affection, before turning to Meg and hugging her as well.

For the first time in her life, she felt as if she truly had a brother.

And that's when it happened.

That's when Grant Sheppard walked into the room.

Three

Grant Sheppard hated this stuff. Obviously, he wanted children to have hope. He just didn't see why a bunch of rich bastards needed to spend fifty thousand dollars to throw a party that would ultimate raise only seventy-five thousand dollars. It didn't make financial sense, and was a damn annoying way to spend an evening.

Besides that, the Children's Hope Foundation annual gala was inevitably overrun by Cains. Which was both one more thing to hate and the only reason he actually bothered to come. There were plenty of stupid charity events he avoided altogether. He came to this one because he didn't want anyone imagining they scared him away.

Though generally he did avoid them. Ostensibly because of the decades-old rivalry between the two families. But he had a more personal reason: he couldn't ever see one of the Cains without thinking of Meg. Sweet Meg. The only woman he'd ever even come close to loving.

Meg, who tasted like sugar and smelled like spices and who—for one brief moment—had held his heart in her hands. Meg, who most likely hated him for running out on her in the middle of the night. And who would hate him even more if she knew the truth…

No, he didn't let himself think about Meg very often.

Loving Meg was just one more reason to hate the Cains, even though she was one of them.

The rivalry between the Cains and the Sheppards had been going on for nearly twenty years, ever since Hollister had edged Russell Sheppard out of the business their fathers had started. There were some things a man never recovered from. Being screwed over by your best friend, your business partner, your mentor…that was one of them. And Grant's father had never recovered. Oh, he'd stumbled along for another decade, but he'd never been the same.

For all intents and purposes, Hollister Cain had destroyed Russell Sheppard. And Grant had vowed to do the same to Hollister and all of his family in return. After years of carefully orchestrated moves, Grant was so close to bringing down Cain Enterprises, he could almost taste it.

Which of course was one more reason he'd come here tonight. Five of the seven board members should be here. All men and women he knew socially and professionally. Soon he would make his move against Cain Enterprises and when he did, he'd need them on his side.

He moved deeper into the room, heading straight for the bar. He didn't drink much, typically. His father's alcoholism had been pretty unappealing to watch. Still, having a drink in his hand gave him something to do while he navigated this shark tank.

The bartender had just handed him his Patron, when a stunning brunette sidled up to him.

"Becca." He smiled and nodded to greet her.

"Grant," she murmured as she rose on her toes to brush a discreet kiss across his cheek and briefly press her body to his. "How are you?"

"Same as always," he said gently.

They had dated briefly a few years ago, before she realized he wasn't interested in marriage. Now she was married to a sixty-three-year-old oil magnate. One of Cain

Enterprises' board members, as a matter of fact. Which worked nicely in Grant's favor, since he got along well with the man.

"I have gossip for you," she said.

"You know I'm not interested in gossip."

"This is about the Cains. And even though you'll hear it soon enough, I desperately want to be the first one to share it with you." She jutted out her lip. "Please."

Grant glanced across the room and saw Becca's husband deep in conversation with one of Houston's congressmen. He turned his attention back to Becca. "You look like you need a drink."

She smiled, clearly delighted that she'd snagged his attention as he headed off to the bar. Five minutes later, he returned with a glass of pinot grigio. Becca actually preferred tequila but never drank it in public. At least, not at this kind of event. Like him, Becca had grown up on the fringes of Houston society. Just rich enough to be included but not rich enough to be an equal. Both of their families had once been old money, but had fallen on hard times. They'd stayed in the social loop, but at the bottom of the pecking order. In so many ways, Becca was his equal. He'd clawed his way back to wealth with ruthless business practices. She'd done it with an advantageous marriage. Neither was particularly proud of their means or motives, but they understood one another. Years ago, he'd thought he and Becca would have been a match made in heaven if they hadn't both been too ambitious to settle for someone as low on the social pecking order as they themselves were. Though, obviously, neither of them was pining away for the other. They were both doing just fine on their own. Which was another reason Becca was perfect for him. There was a lot to be said for a woman he could walk away from without missing.

She took a sip of her drink and smiled blandly. "Thank you."

"And now your news?"

"Do you remember the rumors I told you a few years ago about Hollister losing his marbles when he found out he had a daughter?"

"Of course. He threatened to disinherit all three of his sons unless one of them found her and brought her back to the family."

"Exactly." Becca tapped her hand against his arm, her eyes lighting up with delight. "Which was great news for you. The rumors have gone a long way to destabilizing Cain Enterprises. It doesn't help that Dalton resigned as president and Griffin had to take over."

"Though Griffin has been more competent as president than anyone could have predicted," Grant admitted begrudgingly.

"The point is, Hollister is unstable and losing touch with reality."

"Which I've known for years."

"But that may change, and soon." She leaned forward and whispered. "If you're going to make your move against Cain Enterprises, you need to do it now."

"Why?" The longer rumors circulated about Hollister's poor health and poorer business decisions, the better it would be for Grant.

"Because they found the missing Cain heiress."

For an instant, his heart froze in his chest. Then it started thudding again, slowly. "No. They didn't."

He was sure they hadn't found her. There was no way they could have found her without his hearing about it first.

Those rumors about Hollister having a daughter had spurred his own search for her. Because he had access to his own father's business and personal records from about the time the heiress would have been born, Grant had managed to track Meg down early in the game. He may have initially planned to use her against the Cains, but all that had changed when he'd started to fall for her.

Even though he'd walked away, he felt… proprietary. He'd kept an eye on her. After all, Sheppard Bank and Trust had two locations in Victoria, one of them right across the square from her pie shop. Both the bank manager and the security guards had been told to keep an eye out for anyone from the Cain family—ostensibly because of fears about corporate espionage. Surely he would have heard if the Cain family had been within a hundred yards of Meg and her little pie shop.

He knew the Cains and he knew Meg. Was it really so bad that he wanted to protect her from them?

"Yes, they did." Becca grinned, her gaze lit with malicious glee. "In fact, she's here tonight." Becca nodded in the direction of the dance floor. "Right over there. She was dancing with Dalton the last time I saw her. See for yourself."

"She's here tonight?"

"The whole family is here for her introduction to society." Becca flicked her hair over her shoulder, feigning disinterest. "A little premature, I think. Apparently they just found her this week. And I'd swear that dress she has on is one Portia wore two years ago."

Becca kept talking, but Grant stopped listening. Instead, he gazed over the heads of the crowd, trying to get a look at the woman Becca was talking about.

It wasn't Meg. He knew that much. It just couldn't be.

But—it occurred to him for the first time since he'd left Victoria over two years ago—there might be another heiress somewhere. It was entirely possible that Hollister had fathered more than one bastard daughter he didn't know about. It was possible the Cains had found some other girl who was still Hollister's.

They weren't stupid enough to try to pass off some random woman as his daughter. Not when genetic testing was affordable and the results could be had practically overnight. But there might actually be more than one daughter.

He took a long sip of his tequila and considered. For the past two years, he'd played the long game. He'd planned on the Cains being so involved in this search that he could quietly buy up stock and wait for the company to be rocky enough that he could step in and simply take over. If Hollister died first and disinherited his sons, so much the better.

It had not played out as he'd planned. Hollister was too stubborn to die and Griffin too competent to run Cain Enterprises into the ground.

Still, Grant now owned a healthy chunk of the company. He'd swayed at least three of the seven board members to his side. He almost had it.

And now this.

Some mystery woman messing up his plans.

He excused himself from Becca and started making his way across the room, determined to see just who the Cains had dug up, consoling himself with this one thought: whoever she was, at least their machinations wouldn't hurt Meg.

No matter what happened, no matter how this went down—no matter how he took down Cain Enterprises— at least Meg wouldn't be caught in the cross fire.

Then the crowd parted and he could see the dance floor. He spotted Dalton moving across the floor with a tiny woman in his arms. Her hair, swept up into an elaborate topknot, was dyed a shade of auburn just a little too brassy to be natural. It had one streak of black running through it.

Then Dalton twirled the woman around and Grant got a look at her face.

Shit.

They'd found his Meg.

* * *

Meg was stuck at this interminable party for at least another hour. That's what Portia had told her when Meg demanded to know how much longer she had to stand around like some sort of trophy waiting to be handed off to the winner.

"At ten o'clock the silent auction ends and the live auction begins. That will wrap up by eleven and then there's another two hours of music. You can slip out maybe by 10:10 or so, if Griffin and Sydney are ready to go."

She had begged. They would be ready. But first she had to get through the next hour without catching Grant's eye. She didn't know how exactly she was supposed to do that, when the Cains had orchestrated this entire evening so that everyone in the room would be talking about her.

And no matter where she stood or whom she talked to, she couldn't shut off her awareness that Grant was in the same room. She tried not to look for him, but every time she glanced around the room, there he was. With a series of women, each more beautiful than the next, it seemed. She kept an eye out for lovely blonde mother of his child but didn't see that woman anywhere. Maybe he'd come without her. Which seemed like a real asshole move. Right up his alley then.

There was one woman in particular with whom he spent the most time talking. She had long brown hair and the body of a model.

When Meg couldn't take another moment of talking to strangers, she practically begged Dalton to dance with her.

"Dalton? Dance?" Griffin had scoffed. "If you want to dance, I'll dance with you."

Before she could shoot a pleading look at Dalton, he held out his hand. "No. I'll do it."

A moment later, they were dancing to some staid waltz

she didn't recognize. She breathed deeply, letting go of some of the tension in her shoulders.

After a moment, Dalton asked, "Why didn't you want to dance with Griffin? He is the better dancer."

"He would have wanted to talk," she admitted.

"I take it you're feeling a bit overwhelmed."

"Wouldn't you be?"

Dalton nodded briefly and then said nothing for a while, either because he knew she wanted silence or because he did, she couldn't quite tell. Either way, she was grateful for it. And for the illusion of invisibility that dancing with him gave her. All three of her brothers were tall; surely no one could see her at all when she was hiding behind Dalton.

But then, after what felt like only a few minutes, someone tapped him on the shoulder. "Mind if I cut in?"

At the sound of the man's voice, everything inside her shuddered to a halt. For an instant, she let her eyes drift closed, pretending that she really could disappear. Even when she opened them, she couldn't force herself to look at him.

Dalton guided her just to the edge of the dance floor. "Actually, I do mind," he said to Grant. But he'd stopped dancing and had turned to face the interloper.

"I hear congratulations are in order," Grant said smoothly, ignoring Dalton's rudeness. "You've found your missing sister."

Finally, she made herself meet his gaze. And he was looking directly at her, despite the pretense he made of talking to Dalton. But there was no recognition in his eyes. No surprise or question. If she didn't know better, she'd think he didn't recognize her. But there was no way in hell that could be true.

"We have," Dalton said. He increased the pressure at her back. "Meg Lathem, this is Grant Sheppard, CEO of Sheppard Bank and Trust."

"Pleased to meet you." He held out his hand to shake hers.

Anger kindled inside her at the sight of his hand extended like that. As if they didn't know one another at all. As if he hadn't spent countless nights in her bed. As if he hadn't been deep inside her.

She forced herself to hold out her own hand, braced herself for the impact of feeling his skin against hers for the first time in years.

Much like his tone, his touch was cold and impersonal. "Welcome to Houston."

Dalton, supportive and kind, still had his hand at her back. She smiled brightly. "Thanks, but this isn't my first time here."

His familiar lips twisted in something that was maybe supposed to be a smile. "The band is starting another song. Do you want to dance?"

She was tempted to refuse, but there were so many people watching and she couldn't help thinking this was a test somehow. She would never fit in this world. The world of the Cains and the Sheppards. She wasn't foolish enough to think that.

But for Pearl's sake she needed to at least convince them that she was a Cain.

No Cain had ever been intimidated by anyone or anything. Certainly not a Sheppard.

"You don't have to," Dalton said softly.

"No." She smiled brightly. "I'd love to."

She pushed aside her doubts and fears. She pushed aside all her concerns about Pearl and what she might be doing right now. She even pushed aside the memory from a few days ago of Grant standing outside the Sheppard building with his hand on the waist of the beautiful blonde woman. And the one from just a few moments ago of him standing beside the bar with the brunette.

The man was a hound dog.

She was lucky to have him out of her life and as far away from Pearl as possible. And for the first time in years, she felt relief—genuine relief—that he'd left her in her middle of night and broken her heart. Without hesitation, she stepped into his arms and he whirled her out onto the dance floor. And as long she remembered what a hound dog he was, she wouldn't have to think about how good his arms felt.

"So, Mr. Sheppard, do you enjoy your work in banking?" she asked blandly to keep her hormones distracted.

He stared at her for a second, before increasing the pressure of the hand at her back, pulling her ever so slightly closer. "Is that how we're going to play this?"

"I don't know what you mean."

"You're going to pretend you don't even know me?"

She pulled away, not out of his arms entirely, but enough to put a little more distance between them. "I *don't* even know you."

"Meg," he murmured, dropping his voice to barely a whisper.

"Don't," she said fiercely. "Don't act like you have the right to say my name in that way."

"What way?"

"That sexy, intimate way," she said. His lips curved in a hint of a smile—as if he'd taken it as a compliment—and she had the urge to slap him. She didn't think she'd ever slapped anyone, but she wanted to slap him because he looked so damn confident. As if her words had told him exactly how strongly she still responded to him. As if he knew exactly what was going on in her head, when the truth was, she hardly knew, herself. "Don't act like you know me. You don't."

"I—"

"I am a completely different person than I was then." She laughed as the irony of her words hit her. "Of course, you're not exactly the guy I thought I was falling in love with either. But then again, you never were, were you?"

Something dark and pained flashed through his eyes, giving her the feeling that he had a lot he wanted to say. "It's not in either of our best interests to talk about this here."

"Why? Because your girlfriend might see us or because your wife might hear about it later?"

"My wife? What's that supposed to mean?" But then he shook his head, as though he didn't really want her to answer.

Not that she particularly wanted to talk about it, either. Bringing up the girlfriend and the wife was a huge mistake. It made her seem as if she was still nursing her affection for him. And it potentially revealed that she'd basically been stalking him last week.

Thankfully, the song was coming to an end. In the lull between songs, she stepped away from him abruptly, forcing him to drop his arms. "Thank you for the dance, Mr. Grant. It's been particularly illuminating."

"Wait," he said, reaching out to grasp her arm. "We can't talk here, but we do need to talk. Can I take you to brunch tomorrow? Dinner? Something."

"You're asking me on a date?" Hysterical laughter nearly bubbled up inside her and it was all she could do to control it.

"No," he said seriously, not sensing how close she was to losing it. "Not a date. A conversation."

"No. I'm not getting brunch with you. Or dinner. I wouldn't so much as share a handful of breath mints with you."

He pulled his hand back, tucking it in his pocket, but he didn't turn away from her. He just stood there, looking oddly forlorn on the edge of the dance floor. "There are things we need to talk about."

Aware that they were attracting attention, she stepped just a little closer so no one would overhear her. "You are a lying, cheating bastard. I have nothing to say to you. And there's nothing you could say to me that I would want to hear."

She didn't give him a chance to answer. She knew all too well how charming he could be when he set his mind to it.

But as she walked back across the ballroom to the spot where her family congregated, she wondered if she'd been lying to herself as well as to him.

There were so many things she should be telling him. When she'd first made the decision not to tell him about the baby, it had seemed so logical. So cut-and-dried. Now? Now she wasn't so sure.

Worse still, part of her *did* want to know what he had to say. Part of her would never stop wondering why he'd left.

Four

Cursing under his breath, Grant watched Meg walk away.

What the hell was she doing here?

What. The. Hell.

He had done everything in his power to keep the Cains from finding her. The information from his father that he'd used to find her—he'd buried that deep. He'd made sure no one, not even his stepmother, could find it. Plus, he'd made sure that if the Cains ever did find her, he'd know about it within a matter of hours. She was not supposed to turn up with the Cains at a major social event and catch him by surprise. That was not how this was supposed to go down.

So what the hell had gone wrong?

Becca slithered up next to him, put her hand and head on his shoulder and watched Meg walk away. Then she glanced up at him from under her lashes. "I get the impression that didn't go the way you wanted it to."

"Intuitive, as always," he said dryly.

She gave his shoulder a sympathetic rub. "I guess Hollister's millions of shares of Cain Enterprises stock are going to stay in the Cain family after all."

For an instant, he let his eyes close. For one brief moment, he let himself remember what it had been like to hold Meg in his arms again after all this time. Then, because Becca was there, waiting for an answer, he shifted gears and said, "Not if I can help it."

He watched from across the room as Meg talked first to Sydney and then to Griffin and Dalton. At some point, Portia joined them. He didn't have to hear a word they said to know exactly what was going on. Meg was leaving. Right now. Not later. Not according to whatever plan they'd cooked up before they came. But now.

He could see the determination in her eyes from across the room. Yeah, she was a Cain, all right. But then he'd always known that. He'd always seen that strength in her.

Beside him, Becca rose up on her toes to whisper, "Wanna dance?"

He didn't, but he also didn't want to be rude to Becca. He nodded in the direction he'd last seen her husband. "I don't think Russell would like that."

"Russell is distracted," she murmured, a hint of bitterness in her tone.

Grant scanned the room and quickly found Russell over by the bar, a blonde woman—one younger even than Becca—hanging on his arm and laughing as if he was the funniest guy in the room.

He felt a pang of sympathy for Becca. But he knew her well enough to know that she wasn't a cheater. She might resent the hell out of the bed she'd made for herself, but she would sleep in it until Russell kicked her out.

If Becca could sleep in the bed she'd made, then he'd do the same.

He gave her a buss on the cheek. "Not tonight, darling. Duty calls."

Half hoping to get a chance to talk to Meg alone again, he followed her, Sydney and Griffin out to the front of the hotel. They were closely clustered together, apparently discussing who was going to leave with Meg. Before he could think better of it, he slipped over to the valet stand

and had his car brought around. It was early enough in the evening that the car arrived quickly, so that by the time Dalton handed the driver some money and Meg climbed into a taxicab alone, Grant was waiting in his Lexus just at the end of the circle driveway.

It wasn't stalking to follow her, he told himself. It was caution.

He fully expected the cab to take her back to the Cain mansion in River Oaks, so he was surprised when it headed over to Highway 45 and proceeded south. He was even more surprised when they took an exit on the outskirts of town.

Thirty minutes and what had to be one hell of a cab bill later, they pulled into the parking lot of possibly the crappiest motel in Houston. Between the flickering neon vacancy sign and the occasional boarded-up window, he couldn't believe the place was even still open for business.

But the cab stopped at the far end of the long branch of the L-shaped building, near the staircase, and Meg hopped out. He parked the Lexus and dashed across the pothole-ridden parking lot to her side. He caught up with her by the stairs.

"Jesus, Meg, what are you doing here at this time of night?"

She paused with one foot on the bottom rung of the steps. She blew out a short breath and laughed before pressing her hand to her chest. "Nice, Grant. You scared the crap out of me, running up behind me like that."

He glanced down and saw that she had her purse and hotel key clutched in one hand and pepper spray in the other. He'd come this close to being pepper sprayed. Well, at least she knew enough to be prepared.

He took a step back, holding out his hands in a gesture of innocence.

"Hey, is this guy bothering you?" the cabdriver asked.

He was standing outside his cab now, by the driver's side door, but only one of his hands was visible. "You okay, miss?"

She gave Grant the stink eye for a second before turning a cheerful smile to the driver. "I'm fine. Mr. Sheppard is an old family friend. But thanks for asking."

The driver stared at him, probably long enough to provide an accurate description to a sketch artist, before climbing into the cab and driving off.

Once he was gone, Grant said, "Thank you."

"For what?" She shot him a look as if he was one of the rats scurrying across the parking lot.

"For trusting…" He almost said "me" but changed at the last second to, "…my intentions are good."

She chuckled and headed toward the staircase. "Please. If my dead body turns up in a gutter tomorrow, you're the first person the police would question. So you should be very invested in my safety."

Well. When she put it that way… "Then thank you for at least giving me the chance to talk to you," he said, following her up the stairs to the second floor.

She paused outside one of the rooms that didn't have plywood nailed over the windows. "Who says I'm giving you the chance?"

She jammed a key into the door—an actual metal key, not an electronic key card. Jesus, just how old was this motel? She slipped into the room, but before she could slam the door on him, he slid his shoe into the crack.

"Just five minutes." Great. Now he'd resorted to begging. Fantastic negotiating tactic, begging was.

She eyed his black dress shoe as if it was the cannon of an invading army. Then she met his gaze.

"Five minutes." She muttered the words like a curse as she stepped aside to let him in.

He wouldn't have thought it possible, but the motel

was even worse than he expected. Matted orange carpet covered the floor. His skin crawled just looking at the burnt-orange polyester blanket. Toward the back was a tiny kitchenette with a rust-spotted sink and a stove that might have actually predated the motel itself and looked ready to burst into flames. He felt as if he needed a hepatitis shot just to walk into the place. Or maybe just roach motels strapped to his shoes.

"Jesus, this place is a dump."

She arched a brow, closing the door behind him with restraint. "Welcome to my humble abode."

"Wait. You're not actually living here."

"I am until I leave Houston." She walked past him to the dresser. Facing away from him, she started taking off the glittering jewels that were draped around her delicate wrists and throat.

"You're living here?" he repeated studiedly. "For as long as you're in Houston?"

"That's what I said." For an instant, her gaze met his in the mirror over the dresser. "Now, you can either get in a few more digs about my motel, or you can tell me what you came here to say. You only have four minutes left. Tick tock."

"How long are you going to be staying in town?"

"As long as I need to."

"For what?"

"To convince Hollister I'm his daughter, obviously."

"Did they tell you what they want? Why they need to convince Hollister you're his daughter?"

"Yes, of course." She shot him an exasperated look in the mirror. "They told me all about this quest Hollister sent them on. And all about the money," she said pointedly. "They've been incredibly forthcoming. And quite welcoming, too."

"Of course they've welcomed you. You're their golden

ticket. You're the answer to all their prayers. Now that they have you to present to Hollister, all their money problems are solved." She didn't seem nearly as offended by this idea as he was. He stepped closer, so he was standing right behind her, and spoke more slowly. "They're using you."

She met his gaze in the mirror and he felt himself being pulled toward her. Drawn to her, just as he'd always been.

"They're using me?" she asked, arching an eyebrow.

"Yes."

"They are? That's rich, coming from you."

He ran his hand through his hair in frustration. "Look, I know I haven't done everything right here—"

"Everything?" she asked, and the bitterness in her tone tore at him.

"Okay. I haven't done anything right here. And I know I have absolutely no reason to think I have any say in what you do."

"Good." She whirled to face him. "Because you don't. You have no say. At all."

"But you don't know what you're getting into with the Cains. They are cold and manipulative and—"

"Really, because so far they've been warm and welcoming and totally delightful."

"Welcoming? Is that why you're staying in this crappy hotel out by the highway?"

Her gaze went hard then. Not bitter. Not mean. Just as hard as ice. As brittle too. Her chin bumped up defiantly and she marched right up to him. Even though she barely came to his chin, she managed to glare him down. "I don't take charity from anyone. This crappy hotel out by the highway is what I can afford."

He looked around the room. At the polyester bedspread and the splotchy carpet. At the sink just visible at the back of the room, with its slowly dripping faucet. Anger burned through him, slow and deep. That anger never went away. *This* was what she could afford.

The Cains, collectively, probably had about twenty million dollars in real estate throughout the city. Not counting investments. Just in terms of their homes.

They probably had more guest bedrooms than a European palace. But this was where Meg was staying. Because this was what *she* could afford.

She was standing so close to him, he automatically reached out to grab her arms. For an instant, he was hit again by that powerful urge to pull her to him. To kiss her again. To taste her one more time.

Instead, he pulled her just an inch closer, stared into her eyes and whispered, "You're a Cain now. You can afford to stay anywhere you damn well want to."

She met his gaze head-on. It was different than it had been at the gala, when they were surrounded by people, when the lights were low and the music romantic. There, he'd almost believed she really was a Cain. Almost believed she wasn't the woman he'd once known.

But here, in this crappy motel, under the harsh cheap lights, here he couldn't ignore it. He couldn't pretend. This was Meg. His Meg.

With her alabaster skin and her Cain blue eyes.

She deserved so much better than this. She deserved better than anything the Cains could or would give her. She deserved better than him too.

She glared at him defiantly.

"I am a Cain. I have always been a Cain. And this is where I want to stay."

His gaze dropped to her lips and for a moment the urge to kiss her was almost overwhelming. Would she still taste like cinnamon and sugar? Would she still melt against him?

Before he could find out, she stepped away from him. "I think you should go."

"I don't—"

"Let me rephrase that. I'm done talking to you. And unless you want me to call the police and have your ass hauled out of here, you'll leave."

"Honey, in this part of town, it could be a while before the police get here."

"Then you should save us both the time and leave now."

"This isn't over."

She didn't respond, just stood there gazing at him, defiance in her eyes. "It's been over for more than two years."

Finally, after maybe another minute of staring at her, he turned to leave. "Don't forget to lock the door after me."

"I'm not an idiot."

He looked pointedly around the room. "Right. Despite being a single woman staying alone in an unsafe part of town."

"This feels perfectly safe to me."

"There are drug dealers who wouldn't stay here." She just looked back at him blankly and then eyed the door. He walked out without saying another word.

He'd forgotten how stubborn she was.

He waited outside the door to her motel room until he heard the lock click into place and then he crossed the balcony and went down to his car in the parking lot. He climbed in behind the wheel and locked the door, but didn't drive away. Instead, he eased the seat back and tried to get some sleep. There was no way he was leaving her alone in this part of town. It was going to be a long night.

Five

Despite her late—and mostly sleepless—night, Meg woke up early. Too many years of getting up before dawn to bake for the shop. It was biologically impossible for her to sleep late.

But here, in Houston, in this strange hotel, in this strange town, she could do none of the things she normally did when she woke early. It wasn't as if she was going to bake in the tiny kitchenette. And she'd left her car at the Cains' house last night, so she couldn't even go anywhere until she called a cab. She lay on the uncomfortably lumpy mattress for a long time, just mulling. She'd been foolish to think the Cains could introduce her to Houston society without her ever running into Grant. Yes, Houston was one of the biggest cities in the country, but at that level of wealth, it was a small world.

That was a lesson she'd learned the hard way. She'd first met Grant down in Victoria when he'd wandered into her bakery one afternoon. Then another. And another. He was in town "on business," he'd said, which should have tipped her off, because not many people came to Victoria on business, when people came to Victoria on business they usually didn't wear thousand-dollar suits tailored to fit.

Grant hadn't asked her out right away. He'd just come

in for pie every day, slowly charming her into letting down her guard. When he did ask her out, of course she'd done a Google search on him. She'd realized he was rich and from Houston, but at the time, it had never occurred to her that he knew her family—the family *she* didn't even know. It never occurred to her that he'd sought her out because he knew she was a Cain. For goodness' sake, no one knew she was a Cain. Only three people ever had—her grandfather, her mother and her. And two of those three people had taken the secret to the grave.

It simply hadn't occurred to her that he might have any motive for asking her out other than a simmering attraction and a love of pie.

She'd been a fool.

But even though she regretted her foolishness, she didn't regret their affair. How could she? She couldn't regret Pearl, her dear sweet darling Pearl. Pearl was her everything.

After last night, she was more thankful than ever that she'd never told Grant that she was pregnant. That he had a daughter.

When she'd fallen in love with him, she'd thought he was kind and charming and funny. The Grant she'd danced with last night—the one who'd followed her back here— had been arrogant and rude and pushy. And she had a pretty good idea which Grant was the real Grant. And she didn't want this rude, arrogant man anywhere near her Pearl. Thank goodness she'd gone to the Cains for money instead of him!

She sat up in bed, pulling her knees to her chest and wrapping her arms around them. Chin on her knees, she stared at the dress she'd borrowed from Portia, which she'd hung off the top of the closet door after she'd changed last night. As beautiful as the dress was, as beautiful as she'd looked in the dress, she'd be so glad to be rid of it. It wasn't her. Nothing about last night was her.

The real Meg belonged back in Victoria, baking in the kitchen with Pearl playing nearby and longtime customers sitting at the counter eating her food.

Soon her life would be back to normal.

All she had to do was get through the next few days. The results of the DNA tests would be back on Monday. Hollister would be back from Vail on Tuesday. She only had to get through two more days with the Cains and one awkward meeting with her father and she'd be done with this. She'd be heading back to Victoria with the money she needed to pay for Pearl's surgery. Then everything could go back to normal.

She quietly got out of bed, showered and changed, and then puttered around on her laptop until she heard sounds from the motel room next to hers. As crappy as this motel was—and Grant had been right about that, it was crappy—at least she was only staying here a few days. An entire family lived in the room next to hers. They rented by the week and had been staying there for two months. Five people in one room. Her life might seem complicated right now, but at least she had options. And she had a lot more than some people.

She grabbed her purse—not her real purse, which she had left at the Cain mansion when she'd gotten dressed there the night before—but the sparkly little clutch Portia had loaned her. She scooped the necklace and bracelet off the dresser and carefully tucked them into the purse's sole pocket. The diamond earrings she carefully wrapped in a tissue and tucked into her pants pocket.

Then she left her room, locking up behind her and went to knock next door. A moment later, Mrs. Moreno answered the door, a rosy-cheeked baby on her hip.

Meg smiled at Mrs. Moreno and asked in clumsy Spanish, *"Está Chuy aquí?"*

Mrs. Moreno smiled and nodded, calling out toward the bathroom. Through the partially open door, Meg could see two of the kids still asleep in bed. A moment later, Chuy came out, tucking a shirt into his low-rider jeans.

He was a lanky, teenage boy, wiry and tough, with more pride than men twice his age. Meg didn't know where Mr. Moreno was, or if there even was one, but she'd talked to both of the middle children—Joey and Rosa—several times. She'd befriended them with cookies and coloring books. Chuy was a harder nut to crack. He eyed her a little suspiciously, but ran his hand over his close-cropped hair and nodded. *"Cómo estás?"*

"Hey." She answered in English because her Spanish was crap but his English was fine. "I just wanted to thank you for helping out with my car yesterday."

He looked as if he was about to shrug it off, then glanced behind her. "What's with the suit?"

She looked over her shoulder and nearly cursed. There was Grant. Still dressed in his tuxedo pants and shirt from last night. Except everything was rumpled. Even his hair. As if he'd just rolled out of bed. Not that he looked sexy like that or anything.

She held up a finger to Chuy. "Hang on a minute." And then she crossed the balcony and cut Grant off by her room. "What are you doing here?"

"You're up early."

"What. Are you. Doing here?"

He smiled grimly. "You're the one who said I should be invested in your safety." He gestured toward the parking lot, where she now noticed a silver Lexus was parked. "Consider me invested."

"You slept in your car?" Her mind boggled. She could

even… "Just give me a minute." She waggled her finger at him, glaring. "Stay."

"I'm not a dog," he said.

"Lucky you. Dogs that sleep in parking lots get picked up by Animal Control."

She turned back to Chuy, who was looking way too amused. She walked back over to where Chuy stood, hoping that Grant would give them privacy but suspecting he wouldn't. The man was too pushy.

"Like I said, I just wanted to thank you for fixing my car yesterday." She tried to angle her body to leave Grant out of the conversation. Somehow she just knew he was going to mess this up.

"It was nothing," Chuy said.

"No. You really saved me." She dug the earrings out of her pocket. "I can't pay you in cash, but I have these earrings—"

"He fixed your car?" Grant interrupted.

"Yes, he—"

"It was just a loose radiator hose," Chuy explained. "No biggie."

"Well," she tried again. Gently. Trying to hand the earrings to Chuy. "It was a very big deal to me. So I want to—"

Grant took the earrings from her hand. "Are these the earrings you had on last night?"

"Yes." She glared at Grant and took them back. "Portia gave them to me as a memento. Now I'm using them to pay off my debt to Chuy here."

"Just for attaching a radiator hose?"

"And I was going to ask him to drive me downtown, since I left my car at Portia's house."

Grant grabbed the hand with the earrings and pulled Meg a step away. "You can't give a kid like this diamond earrings."

"Why not?"

"For starters, if he walks into a pawnshop and tries to sell them, he's not going to get what they're worth. And he'll probably get arrested." He glanced at Chuy. "No offense."

"None taken." Chuy shrugged, smiling almost shyly at Meg. "I wouldn't have taken them anyway. But thanks."

She let out a frustrated sigh and opened her mouth to argue, but before she could say anything, Grant pulled out his wallet. She watched in astonishment as he thumbed through it and extracted some bills.

"Here. Instead of the earrings."

Chuy eyed Grant for a moment then accepted the cash.

This time, Meg really did throw up her hands. "What, you'll take money from him but not from me?"

Chuy laughed. "If you had enough money, then yeah, I'd take it from you. And if you've got friends with this much cash, you shouldn't be staying in a dump like this." Then he pointed a finger at Grant and scolded. "Why are you letting her stay here? Take her someplace safer."

And before she could say anything else, Chuy slipped back into the hotel room. As frustrated as she was that he wouldn't accept money from her and that there wasn't more she could do to help him, she knew she had to let this one go.

But now she had no ride back downtown. Unless she wanted to call Portia. And feel even more beholden to them. Even that would be better than riding with Grant.

Grant took her arm in his and started guiding her back toward her room. "Come on. Let's grab your stuff and get out of here."

"I'm not—"

He stopped and turned her to face him. He looked at her, his gaze serious and intense. "I'm not ordering you. I'm not pushing you around. This is me asking you. Please, for the sake of my back and my sanity. Please let me take you someplace else."

Humiliation burned through her. Where exactly did he think she had to go?

Then almost as if he'd read her mind—damn him—he added, "If you really don't have the money, then for God's sake ask the Cains."

"No way." That was an exercise in humiliation she didn't feel like preforming.

"Then let me put you up at a hotel."

Hysterical laughter bubbled up. "Right. The missing Cain heiress is finally discovered. Hotelled at the expense of the Cains' worst enemy. That would go over well. Dalton looked like he was going to have an aneurism when we danced together last night. You really think—"

"I wasn't exactly planning on asking his permission. But if he's half as decent as you keep saying he is, then he'd do more than have an aneurism if he saw this motel. If you don't want to accept charity from them or from me, then pawn the damn earrings yourself and use that to cover your hotel."

Shoving a lock of hair out of her face, she looked down the length of the motel balcony. It really was a crap motel. And the only reason she was stubbornly clinging to the idea of staying here was because it seemed like…oh, hell, she didn't know. Like that last bit of herself she was clinging to. Like the second she checked out of here and let Grant or the Cains or anyone else put her up in a nicer place, she'd be giving them some level of control over her life.

But that was unavoidable. She'd known that from the beginning. From the moment she'd packed up her car, kissed Pearl on the check and headed for Houston. She'd known that if she came here, she was handing her life over to someone with more money and power than she had. She wondered if the Cains were really any better than Grant. But at least they didn't have the power to hurt her.

She put the earrings back in her pants pocket, shoving

them deep inside, and took her motel key out of the other pocket. "Okay. I'll check out and…figure something out later." She unlocked the door, trying to slip in, but Grant caught it and held it open.

"Pack up your stuff. I'll be waiting outside."

Yeah. That was what she was afraid of.

Ten minutes later, she slid her suitcase into the trunk of his Lexus and carefully draped the bag containing Portia's dress over it.

When she climbed into the passenger seat, he asked, "Okay. Where to?"

"I don't suppose you'll consider just dropping me at the next cheap motel?" He didn't so much as crack a smile. "Okay. Portia's." She rattled off the address, then settled into the seat, propping her elbow by the window and staring out. "You know, I remember you having a better sense of humor."

"Yeah," he agreed grimly. "Well, great sex does a lot to improve a man's sense of humor."

She slanted a look at him. She hadn't expected him to bring that up. He didn't even glance in her direction but kept his gaze focused on the road.

Yes, things had been explosive between them when they'd been together before. Once she'd given in and agreed to a date, it had been…like nothing she'd ever felt before. Would it still be like that?

She studied his hands. The restrained but controlled way he gripped the steering wheel. His fingers were long and his hands were strong. Not soft, as she'd expect a banker's to be, but tough.

She shivered, remembering his touch. He liked being in control and she'd loved making him lose it.

Yes, it would still be like that. She was still so damn vulnerable to him.

Six

After that, they spent most of the drive in silence. She'd rattled off Portia and Cooper's address and then turned to sit with her arms folded over her chest, staring out the window. Giving him nothing.

He slowed down as he drove through Portia's neighborhood. Once she got out of this car, she'd vanish from his life again. Maybe forever. Maybe it would be for the best. She certainly didn't need him in her life. She never had.

Except for the fact that her life wasn't her own anymore. She belonged to the Cains now. She didn't seem to realize it yet, but her life had changed forever. He knew better than anyone how vulnerable she was. How damn naive.

And somehow, miraculously, being screwed over by him hadn't seemed to change that. She was still the same gentle, trusting person she'd been before their affair. The debacle with the earrings this morning proved that. How was it that she still didn't understand how the world worked? That she still didn't know that people would take advantage of her every damn chance they got.

"How the hell are you still so trusting?" he asked, breaking the silence.

"I don't trust *you*, that's for sure. I thought that was obvious when I threatened to have you arrested."

"Great. Don't trust me. I'm not asking you to. But the Cains? That kid at the motel?"

"Chuy Moreno. Chuy and his family were always kind to me. The Cains have also been nice."

"You can't just trust—"

But she held up her hand and cut him off. "One rich asshole screwed me over. I'm not going to let that dictate how I live the rest of my life." Her voice took on a hard note of determination. "I'm not going to let you make me distrustful and cynical. I refuse to be like—"

She broke off abruptly.

After a second, he finished the sentence for her. "You don't want to be like your mother." She'd said that before. Over two years ago when they were together. At the time he hadn't pressed the issue, but now he did. "After what Hollister did to your mother."

"What do you know about that?" She turned to look at him sharply.

"Everything. I think. He was business partners with my father about the time you were conceived. My father had a journal, so I think I've pieced it together. Besides, I know how he treated women. My stepmother, the woman who raised me, was involved with Hollister before she married my dad. I know better than anyone what he did to—"

"I will not talk about Hollister with you. Ever." She sliced her hand through the air as if she were trying to erase his words. "And for the record, I was going to say that I refuse to be like *you*."

Well. He guessed he had *that* coming. He was silent until he'd reached the address Meg had given him. The house was not the mansion he expected but a modest bungalow, even though the neighborhood was a nice one. He might have doubted he was in the right place, except he saw Meg's Chevy sitting out front. The thing had been a

POS when they'd first met. He could hardly believe it was still running.

He put the car in Park and twisted to face her. "What I did, it was a real asshole move. I'm not going to pretend it wasn't."

She just stared at him, eyebrows raised, as if she was surprised he'd admit it.

"Oh, that's generous. I'm glad you're so in touch with your assholery."

"Look, when I showed up in Victoria, I had a clear plan. Seducing you was all part—"

"I was there, remember?" She cut him off. Her tone was flippant and breezy. Way breezier than he felt right now. "You don't need to tell me what happened. We were together for two months and then you just disappeared in the middle of the night. No note. No phone call. Nothing. I don't need the play-by-play."

"Okay. No play-by-play. But I need you to understand why I did it."

"Why? So then you don't have to feel guilty about it anymore? No, thank you. If you want absolution, you'll have to find it someplace else."

"No, that's not what I want." Christ, he knew he didn't deserve absolution. And he certainly wouldn't ask her for it. "You need to know what people like me are capable of. The Cains are like me. They will do whatever it takes to get what they want. They will use you and manipulate you."

"And you think I'm just too stupid to protect myself? Maybe I am. But guess what? I'm not your problem. If I get hurt, it's not your problem. If the Cains manipulate me, it's not your problem. Nothing I do has anything to do with you. You are officially and completely absolved of any responsibility."

Before he could stop her, she hopped out of the car and

strode around to the back. When he didn't pop the trunk right away, she slapped her hand on it.

Jesus. What was he supposed to do now? Just let her walk into enemy territory? Just let her get screwed over one more time? Just stand by and watch that happen? Because he was not okay with that. He would never be okay with it.

Instead of popping the trunk from the driver's seat, he climbed out of the car and went around to the back. Ignoring her glare, he handed her the dress and took out the rolling suitcase himself.

She just stood there, staring up at him. Her blue eyes narrowed in disdain, her brow furrowed as she held out her hand for him to give her the handle of her suitcase. This was it. The last time he'd ever need to talk to her. It was officially over.

"Take care of yourself. If you ever need—"

"I won't." She grabbed the handle from him and yanked the suitcase up onto the curb. She was halfway up the walkway to the house when the front door opened and Portia came out onto the porch. She was dressed in simple jeans and T-shirt. She frowned for a second when she saw him, then ducked back inside the house. A moment later, Cooper came out onto the porch.

Like the rest of the world, Grant had thought it strange when Portia and Cooper had gotten married six months ago. But he'd never really had a problem with Cooper. The way he saw it, when it came to the Cains, Cooper had gotten an even shorter end of the stick than Grant had.

So he was shocked when Cooper stormed down the pathway toward him, fury written all over his face.

"What's up—?" he started to ask, but before he could get the whole question out, Cooper pulled back a fist and decked him. Stumbling back into the street, Grant brought his hand to his face. "What the hell?"

Cooper followed him, grabbing the front of his shirt and swinging him around to push him up against the side of the car. "You screwed with my sister."

Cooper punched him again.

Yeah, this time he saw the punch coming and he just took it. Fair was fair. He had screwed with Meg. If Cooper wanted to get in a couple of punches, Grant deserved it. It was what he would do if anyone screwed with his sister the way he'd screwed with Meg.

"You bastard," Cooper growled.

Still, he wasn't just going to let Cooper beat the crap out of him. He took another hit to the stomach before deflecting Cooper's next blow and ducking under his arm. He moved just beyond Cooper's reach and held up his hands to try to calm Cooper down. "Hang on, be reasonable. I—"

"You got her pregnant and then abandoned her."

"What?" Shock rooted him in place. Cooper hauled back and hit him again. Square on the jaw. And this time he went out.

Seven

Grant woke up on a sofa with a bag of frozen peas on his head. It took several head-splitting, foggy minutes to orient himself. He couldn't think beyond the thudding in his brain and the sweet smell of cinnamon and the warm, soft touch of fingers on his head.

It was the smell of comfort and peace.

It was the smell of Meg.

Slowly, it all came back to him. Meg was in Houston. With the Cains. And he'd tried to warn her about them, except Cooper had come out of the house and punched him. And claimed Grant had gotten Meg pregnant.

At that, he forced his eyes open despite the pain.

There she was, leaning over him. She sat on the edge of the sofa that he'd been laid out on, her hip pressing into his. He could only assume that he was in Portia and Cooper's house. That Cooper had carried him in after knocking him out. But he didn't see Portia or Cooper in the living room. Meg's eyes had a worried expression as she held the peas in place.

He grabbed her wrist. "Was Cooper right?"

She didn't quite meet his gaze. "I don't know how he found out about us. I didn't tell him. I—"

"Is Cooper right? Were you pregnant when I left?"

"What does it matter?" She pulled her wrist out of his grasp and stood.

"It matters." He pushed himself up, swinging his legs around and forcing himself to sit despite the ringing in his ears. "Do I have a child? Did you—?" He let the question hang, because he didn't know how to ask.

She stood up and turned her back on him. "I have a daughter. I do."

"Is she mine?"

She whirled around, glaring at him. "No," she hissed. "She's my daughter. Mine."

"Is. She. Mine?"

"No."

But now Meg wasn't meeting his gaze.

In that instant, she didn't have to. He'd seen it in her eyes. Yes, they had a child together. If the circumstances had been different, if she'd come to him with this news, he might have questioned her. He might have demanded a paternity test. Instead, she'd tried to keep the news hidden, which did more to convince him the baby was his than anything else could have.

Cooper had obviously known the truth about him and Meg. And Cooper thought the baby was his.

No. Not *baby*. He and Meg had been together more than two years ago. The baby would be a toddler now. A little girl.

A little girl. He had a child. A daughter.

Maybe.

The ringing in his ears got louder as blood pounded in his head. It was all he could do to hold his head in his hands. Then he stood and looked around the room. Meg still had her back to him, her arms wrapped around her waist. She wasn't talking.

The living room led into a dining room and there was a door on the far wall, which he guessed led to the kitchen. He headed for that door and sure enough, there were Cooper and Portia, standing together, whispering. Grant stopped just inside the doorway and waited until they looked up.

"Is the child mine?" he asked.

Meg came up behind him and pushed past him.

From the corner of his eye, he could see her give a slight shake of her head.

Portia, watching Meg, frowned, bringing her hand up to cover her mouth. "Oh, Meg. You didn't tell him."

Cooper looked from one to the other of them, as if he didn't know what to say. As if he didn't know whose side to be on. He just shook his head and finally said, "When she came to us and needed all that money, hiring a PI seemed like a no-brainer. We didn't get the info about Pearl until this morning."

Beside him, he could feel the moment Meg gave up, the moment all the tension left her body and she resigned herself.

Grant turned back to her. "Pearl?" he asked. "Her name is Pearl?"

Meg glared at him.

"You have a daughter…we have a daughter named Pearl. And you never bothered to mention this fact to me."

He saw the instant of indecision in her eyes. That moment she decided whether or not to try to justify her decision or come out with her guns blazing.

"No. I didn't mention it to you. And you know why I didn't? Because you weren't there. Because one night, in the middle of the night, you just disappeared. No note. No phone call. Nothing. You could have been dead, for all I knew. In fact, I thought you must have been dead, because I couldn't conceive of you leaving like that. I actually thought you must have gotten a call back to Houston and died on the road. That's how sure I was that you wouldn't just up and leave in the middle of the night. So, yeah, then I realized that I was wrong about you, that you didn't love me, that you had never loved me, that you had every reason in the world to hate me and hate the Cains and to want us to suffer. And then three months later when I found out I was pregnant…" She gave a bitter, maniacal laugh. "Yeah. What do you think?"

For a second, all he could do was picture her. Alone. In her tiny house. Waiting for him. Worrying about him. Imagining him dead. And then figuring out the truth. Which, in her mind, was probably worse than finding out he was dead.

In that moment, when he thought about it like that, he could almost believe that her actions were justified. Almost.

Except for the fact that he had a daughter. He had flesh and blood that he had never known about. And…

"Wait." He turned to look at Meg. "Why do you need money?" He grabbed her by the arms. From the corner of his eye, he saw Cooper take a step toward him and he automatically let her go, pissed all over again. "Why do you need money?"

Meg just glared at him. "What does it matter to you? She's nothing to you."

"I didn't even know she existed." He wanted to grab her again. To shake her. To make her make sense, but he was painfully aware of Cooper standing just off to the side. Ready to step in. "Why do you need money?" he demanded again.

It seemed so obvious now. Of course she needed money. Why else would she have come to the Cains otherwise? Obviously she had figured out, or had always known, what no one else had. That she was Hollister's daughter. And, equally obviously, she never would have come to them unless things were bad. Really bad.

"Why do you need the money?" he repeated.

Meg's eyes narrowed and from the stubborn tilt to her chin, he could tell that she had no intention of actually answering.

He whirled toward Portia. "Why does she need the money?"

Portia just looked at him, her eyes wide and uncertain. She glanced from him to Meg, biting her lip and looking as if she didn't know how to handle this.

"Pearl has a congenital heart defect from Down syndrome. She needs surgery." It was Cooper who answered. "I'm sorry, Meg. He had to find out eventually."

For a second, Grant's mind raced so fast and so hard he almost couldn't breathe. His daughter had Down syndrome. He couldn't even think about that right now. Not when the rest of the bomb was still shaking his foundation. A congenital heart defect.

His daughter—the child he hadn't even known about until five minutes ago—needed heart surgery.

He remembered the fear and anguish he'd felt as a kid when his father went in for heart surgery. That had been terrifying. How much worse would it be if it was his kid?

He turned back to Meg. "My daughter—who I never even knew about—needs heart surgery and instead of coming to me, you went to them? What the hell were you thinking?"

But apparently Meg was done being cowed, because she bumped up her chin and stepped into the fight. "What was I thinking? I was thinking you'd abandoned me. I was thinking you didn't give a damn what happened to me, seeing as how you'd disappeared from my life and never—not once—bothered to contact me or check on me. Seeing as how the only reason you seduced me in the first place was to—" She broke off, gesturing broadly. "I don't know. What? This is the part I've never figured out. What was the plan? To somehow get at Hollister through me? But then you realized Hollister didn't even know me and certainly didn't give a crap about me, so you just left. Once I figured that out, how eager do you think I was to hunt you down and let you know you were a father?"

Her accusations burned through his chest. And he couldn't even defend himself against them because the truth—the real reason he'd seduced her—was worse. "You didn't tell me you were pregnant, fine. But as soon as she was born, as soon as you realized she had health problems that you couldn't afford, you should have come to me then. You should have set aside your pride and come to me."

"Are you serious? You think I'd let my pride get in the way of Pearl's health?"

"Isn't that what you did? She's nearly eighteen months now. And if she needed a surgery that you couldn't afford—"

Meg slapped him across the cheek. And then she got right in his face and spoke in a low, furious whisper. "Pearl's doctor wanted to wait. Yes, she needs the surgery. Eventually. The doctors didn't even decide until two weeks ago that she definitely needed the surgery. I cannot believe you think I'd put my ego before her health. I can't believe you'd accuse me of that."

"You should have come to me first for the money before going to them."

"I *did* come to you first. As soon as I found out she needed the surgery, I came to you. But there you were with your wife and your baby girl. And I just couldn't go to you. Not when I had another option."

"My what? What are you talking about? I don't have a wife. I don't have a daugh—" But he broke off midword. "The only daughter I have is *your* daughter."

"No," she said, almost frantic. "Just last week. I came to Houston. To see you and tell you about Pearl. And I saw you with them, a woman and a baby. Trust me, you looked very close."

"Trust me. She's not my wife. If I had a wife I would know it. Of course, until ten minutes ago, I would have said the same thing about a daughter, but I guess I was wrong about that."

"She's blonde. You were out in front of Sheppard Bank and Trust. Around noon. And trust me, if she's not your wife, she's someone you're very close to."

"Yeah. I am close to her. She's my sister, Grace. That baby, Quinn, is my niece. Which I happily would have told you if hadn't been looking for reasons not to tell me the truth."

"I wasn't looking for reasons. I just couldn't tell you about Pearl. Not when that baby was so—" Meg broke off sharply.

"So," he said, understanding dawning, "you're ashamed of our daughter."

"No! Pearl is amazing. But she's different." Meg glared at him. "And not every parent—not every parent—can easily accept that. My instinct is always going to be to protect her when I'm not sure how someone is going to react. You don't know what that's like."

"No. You're right," he said bitterly. "I don't know what it's like. But that's going to change. Right now. I want to meet her."

Everything in Meg rebelled at the idea of Grant meeting Pearl.

Her wonderful, perfect, amazing Pearl. He couldn't meet her. Not yet. He wouldn't understand. He wouldn't know how to act with her. And seeing them together, seeing Pearl's sweet loving nature, seeing Grant's clumsy attempts to not feel awkward would kill Meg.

"No!" she said quickly. Her gut response.

"Meg—" he said in a low, threatening voice.

"Not like this. Not when you're so angry." Not when he wasn't prepared. "Not now."

"Yes. Now. I want to meet her. Today."

"Just give me some time to set something up. Give me—"

But he'd stopped listening. He just turned and walked out.

She stared after him, her heart pounding and her mouth suddenly dry. When she heard the front door slam, all the fight went out of her. The stress and exhaustion of the past two weeks suddenly bore down on her, crushing her.

She sank into a nearby chair, burying her head in her hands. "This is a disaster!"

Portia came to sit next to her, rubbing her shoulder as if she was soothing a child. "I'm so sorry. We didn't realize he didn't know about Pearl."

Meg turned to look at Portia. "Why did you hire the PI? Why not just ask me?"

"I'm sorry," Portia said. "You were so prickly about the money at first. We were worried."

"We all agreed to it," Cooper said. "What would you have us do? You came to us saying you needed two hundred thousand dollars, but you didn't want to answer our questions. We couldn't just give you the money."

She sat up straight. "You weren't going to give me the money?"

"Not until we knew why you needed it. For all we knew, you were in serious trouble. If you needed our help, we were going to do whatever we had to. Even if it meant not giving you the money. We were trying to protect you. I don't think any of us imagined something like this."

"I'm so sorry," Portia said.

"What am I going to do now?" she asked aloud. Not that she expected an answer. This was a mess and there was no easy way out. Grant would never forgive her. Not that she blamed him. Not that she wanted his forgiveness.

It had never occurred to her that he would want to be a part of Pearl's life. Honestly. It had never once occurred to her.

"I guess I'll give him some time to calm down and then try to talk to him again."

Cooper pushed off from the counter and came to stand by his wife, but he was looking at Meg as he spoke. "Honey, I hate to break it to you, but Grant didn't go somewhere to calm down."

"He didn't?" Portia said.

Meg realized the truth. Inside, she started screaming even as Cooper was answering.

"No. He's going to find her."

"Oh, God," Meg muttered.

"You don't know that," Portia said, no doubt trying to comfort her.

"It's what I would do," Cooper said simply.

In that moment, Meg knew with absolute certainty that Cooper was right. It was what any man would do.

She stood up, her mind racing. She had no doubt that Grant could find Pearl. It was just a matter of time. Victoria was not that big. Her pie shop was right in the center of town. Everyone knew where it was. And everyone knew Pearl. She had no doubt that Janine wouldn't let him see Pearl. But Grant had essentially lived there for months and he had been well liked. People would remember him. Someone would tell him where Pearl was. And Meg didn't want to put Janine in that position.

She had to get to Pearl first.

Eight

He didn't really expect that he would get to Pearl before Meg would. In fact, when he'd left Portia and Cooper's in Houston, he hadn't really had a plan in mind. Just get to Victoria and see Pearl with his own eyes.

Just get there and meet his daughter.

His daughter.

That had been his sole focus. He'd driven like hell to get there. Meg's little bakery, Sweet Things, was right where it had always been, on the town square, across from the back entrance to the county courthouse. But she'd moved out of the bungalow where she used to live. Now a young couple lived there. But thanks to some quick work on his smartphone he was able to track her down via the county tax office to a seventies-style ranch house on the north side of town. It didn't take a genius to figure out which house was hers. It was the only one with a Maserati out in front. The same Maserati that she'd seen in front of Portia and Cooper's. Grant parked his sedan behind Cooper's sports car. No wonder they'd gotten there first.

Meg and Cooper stood on the front porch of the house, but when Grant climbed out of the car, Cooper stepped in front of Meg and met Grant halfway down the path.

Cooper was a big guy—all lean, snowboarder muscle. He was tough, but Grant could take him. "Don't even think about trying to keep me from seeing Pearl or Meg."

"I wasn't going to. I'm just here to remind you that she's not alone. She's not defenseless. And if you try to bully her, you won't succeed. And if you so much as touch her—"

"Understood." The mere suggestion pissed him off even more. Worse still, Grant knew that Cooper had said it because of the way Grant had grabbed her arms earlier. He had never touched a woman in violence. He never would, but some part of him was glad she had someone in her life who would stand up for her, even if it was against him. "Now get out of my way."

Cooper gave a terse nod before going back up onto the porch, planting himself in front of the door. Meg stepped down into the yard, her arms crossed over her chest, her jaw clenched belligerently.

She was tough. No doubt about it. But she was vulnerable too. It was there in the slight quiver of her lips. In the rigidity of her posture. He pushed that awareness away. She may appear vulnerable, but she could clearly be ruthless.

"You know you can't keep her from me," he said simply.

"I'm not going to try. I just want you to think twice before doing this. You have every reason to be mad at me. Fine. Be mad at me. And I know you hate the Cains. Fine. Hate them. But don't drag her into this."

"That's what you think? That I drove down here so I could exact some sort of revenge on you?"

"Isn't it?" Her chin bumped up defiantly.

"I drove down here because I have a child I didn't know about until today. A child I've never met." He leaned down. "The only reason I came here is because I want to meet my daughter."

Meg studied him for a second and then asked, "Are you sure? Are you sure you're ready to be a father? Only a few people know she's your daughter. You could just walk away."

"*I* know she's my daughter. I'm going to do what's right by her."

Meg's gaze hardened. "What makes you so sure this is it? Do you really think she's going to benefit from this momentary sense of guilt and obligation you're feeling?"

"You think I'm only here because I feel guilty?"

"Yeah. I do."

"You're wrong."

"Then why *are* you here?"

"Because she's mine."

Before she could say anything else, Cooper spoke from his spot on the porch. "She's right."

Grant looked to see Cooper standing there, arms crossed over his chest as he propped a shoulder against the supporting column. "I didn't ask you."

"No. But of the three of us, I'm the one who had to put up with Hollister's disinterested, half-assed, lazy fathering. It would have been infinitely better for me and my mother if he hadn't been there at all."

Meg frowned, looking at her brother with a mix of sympathy and affection. And understanding.

Which was just great. Because that meant, in this little scenario, he was playing the Hollister role.

Hollister Cain was the greediest, most manipulative SOB Grant had ever met.

And these two people—one of whom had been an acquaintance for most of his life and the other of whom had claimed to be in love with him—both thought he was as bad as Hollister.

That was just fantastic news.

Of course, the problem was that he didn't necessarily disagree. And he had the feeling they were going to like what was coming next even less.

"If you're done maligning my character, I'd like to meet my daughter. After all, we have a long day ahead of us. And it's a long drive back to Houston."

Anger and frustration boiled together inside her, emulsifying into some new, awful emotion.

Why did he have to make this so hard? Why couldn't he let it go?

"See? This! This is exactly what I didn't want to happen." If she could just make him understand what a huge mistake this was. For everyone. "Pearl doesn't need you to come down here and play daddy for the day. I don't need it. And you don't need it, either. Why not just walk away?"

"You think I'm just playing at this?"

"I think you haven't thought it through. What good will it do anyone for you to meet Pearl today and then disappear from her life all over again?"

A slow, humorless smile spread across his face. "Oh, I have no intention of seeing Pearl only for today."

Wait. What?

Warning bells rang in her ears, but she still couldn't put it all together. "But you said you were going back tonight."

"No." He took a step closer to her so he was looming over her. "I said it was a long drive. A drive we're all going to make together. You. Me. And Pearl. You're both coming back to Houston with me."

"What?"

"You. And Pearl." He spoke more slowly this time, his gaze never once wavering from hers. "Are coming back. To Houston. With me."

For one endless moment, she felt skewered by his gaze. By the absolute, sheer will in his eyes. She'd once thought he knew her better than anyone else. She'd once given him her heart and her body. Her everything. And if she had to see him every day, she might be tempted to do so again. Would she be strong enough to resist him?

"We can't go to Houston with you. We live here."

"Not anymore you don't."

"I don't..." Her words stuttered to a stop as her brain tried to keep up. "I can't..." There were so many reasons. Her job. The bakery. Her friends. Everyone she'd ever known. "That's ridiculous!"

"What's ridiculous is that I have a daughter I've never met and we're still standing out on the street talking about this."

"I have a job! I have a business! I can't just move to Houston."

"You were already planning on being in Houston at least another week. So whoever is running the bakery can just keep running it," he pointed out, his voice so cool and logical it drove her crazy. "You'll extend the trip. One month. At least."

"I can't stay in Houston for another month! I can't afford it."

"Of course you can. You and Pearl will move in with me."

"No!" she protested. Move in with Grant? She couldn't live with Grant for a month. Or even a week. Hell, just dancing with him last night had made her all trembly inside. A week living in the same house with him would leave her a wreck.

"Yes. Because you can sure as hell bet I'm not letting you pick where you stay. My daughter isn't going anywhere near that dump."

"Pearl's doctors are here. Her surgeon is here. We can't just—"

"I guarantee, the surgeons in Houston are better. I started calling in favors on the drive down. Pearl has an appointment Monday morning with the best pediatric cardiologist in town. He's one of the best in the country."

And again, there was nothing she could do but stutter. Her life was spinning wildly out of control. Grant was like the industrial mixer she had in the bakery. It was so strong, it scared her sometimes. It made amazing meringues. Incredible whipped cream. It did exactly what it was made to do and it did it well. It was a thing of beauty and violence. There was something so hypnotic about watching it. She almost feared she'd tumble right in, like Alice into the rabbit hole. Grant was like that. Hypnotic. Powerful. Destructive.

"I won't let you do this," she said desperately. "I won't let you just take control of my life. I'll fight you if I have to."

His smile broadened. "You want a legal fight? Bring it. I will bury you. I will bury you so deep, you'll never climb out."

She felt his scorn, his anger, his bitterness like a physical thing. Like a weight pressing down on her chest. His sheer determination was almost terrifying.

He would do it. If she refused to bring Pearl to Houston, if she refused to move in with him for the next month, he would sue for custody. Oh, he'd stopped just shy of saying that's what he was going to do, but the implication was there.

How could she even respond to that? She could barely breathe. Forget talk. Forget logic or reason or common sense.

She started begging. "At the very least, give me time to talk to her first. Don't meet her like this. Don't meet her when you're so angry."

Cooper must have realized she was floundering, because he stepped up, placing his hand on her shoulder as he passed as if he were tapping her out of a wrestling ring.

Then he stepped in front of her. "Back off, Sheppard. I told you already. You can't bully her. She's not alone anymore. You pick a fight with her, you pick a fight with all of us."

For several tense heartbeats, the two men just stood there, staring one another down. Her brother was tall and lean with the build of a lifelong athlete. If someone had asked her a few days ago, she would have sworn Cooper could win any fight he got into. But looking at Grant now, taking in the cold determination in his gaze, the way he clenched and unclenched his fists, she wasn't sure. He looked as if he could barely control the urge to knock out Cooper. As if the punch was dancing along his nerve endings and only a tremendous will was holding it back.

Then, abruptly, Grant glanced at her. All that emotion hit her like a blow to the solar plexus. There was nothing in his gaze but cold determination and it still hit her hard. Because no matter what he'd done, a part of her still wanted him. Maybe a part of her always would.

For a second he studied her. Then he took a step back. "Pack your bags and get our daughter ready to go. I will be back here in one hour."

Then he turned on his heel and walked away. The instant his Lexus squealed around the corner, all the tension rushed out of Meg.

She sank to the step and buried her head in her hands. "Oh, Lord. What am I going to do? What am I going to do?"

She just sat there, muttering the question over and over again. Because—honest to God—she did not know what to do about this.

And then she felt Cooper's hand on her shoulder, heard the creak of old wood as he lowered himself to the step beside her. "I meant what I said to Sheppard. You're not alone. You say the word, we'll fight him."

She twisted to look at Cooper. This guy she'd only met less than a week ago. This guy who couldn't possibly care about her. Yet somehow, he seemed to.

She'd been on her own so long. Sometimes it seemed like her whole life. Her mother had died when she was little. Her grandfather had had a very laissez-faire attitude about raising her. Yes, he'd loved her, but he'd spent a lot of time living in his head. He'd trusted her to be smart enough and independent enough to take care of herself. Yes, she had tons of friends now. Most days, it felt as if the lifeblood of Victoria pumped through her little bakery. In so many ways, the entire town was her family. But she would never—never—ask them to back her up in a fight.

Would she ask that of the Cains?

She's spent much of her life sneering at their wealth and privilege. Disdainful of their shallow, money-grubbing lives. But her brothers and their wives were not who she'd thought they were. They'd welcomed her. They'd been kind to her. And they *felt* like family.

Which would make it both easier and harder to rely on them.

"I just don't know," she admitted. She looked up at Cooper. "How serious do you think he is?"

Cooper met her gaze for a moment, and then looked off down the street, considering his answer. "I don't know Grant well. Dalton or Griffin might have a better read on him. They've known him forever. Went to the same schools. Traveled in the same circles. They were never friends because Sheppard has hated the Cains forever, but they'd be able to read him better." He paused, and she thought that was all he was going to say. Except then he glanced back at her and added, "But if it was me, if I was in his shoes, I'd be pretty damn serious."

She dropped her head back in her hands. Christ. What a mess.

How had she not considered this?

Because she honestly thought Grant wouldn't give a fig about having a daughter. Even when she'd decided to go to him for the money for Pearl's surgery, she'd thought it would be a short conversation. One that involved a fair bit of threatening on her part before he forked over some cash to get rid of her. It hadn't occurred to her that he would want to be a part of Pearl's life. That he would care.

"I'm sorry," she said.

"For what?"

"For not realizing that a man would care about something like this, I guess."

Cooper arched an eyebrow. "You don't think men care about their kids?"

"Did Hollister care about you?" she countered. "You're the one who said you would have been better off without him."

"True. But Hollister is a sociopathic bastard. Frankly, it's amazing none of us are more messed up than we are."

She nearly laughed at that, despite the weight in her heart. Because Cooper was certainly right. As far as she could tell, her brothers were all decent, caring guys. Dalton was a bit humorless and cold—except when he was with his wife, Laney, or their baby. Griffin was charming and personable. So charming, in fact, that she might think he lacked sincerity—except when he was with Sydney. She brought out a warmth in him.

But it was Cooper she felt the closest to. He was the other outsider. The other bastard. The other unplanned, unwanted child.

"I never wanted Pearl to feel unwanted," she mused aloud. "I never wanted him to have the chance to reject her, I guess."

"I get that," Cooper said quietly. "Look, I can't tell you what to do."

"But…"

"If nothing else, Houston has very good doctors. Some of the best in the world."

"So you think I should go to Houston with him?"

"I think Pearl is your daughter and you have to decide what to do. The rest of us have your back no matter what. If you want to see the doctors in Houston without him, we'll make it happen. If you want to stay here, we'll make that happen too."

She sighed, staring out at the street beyond her tiny front porch. This was the house she'd grown up in. This was her neighborhood. And except for the few years she'd lived just north of town, she'd been here all her life. Victoria was all she'd ever known. She wasn't used to having options.

But was she really being honest with herself? Was she scared of leaving Victoria because she was afraid living in Houston would overwhelm her or because she was afraid living with Grant would overwhelm her heart?

It had been so much easier to hate him when she's assumed he wouldn't want their daughter.

But in the end, it came down to this: what was best for Pearl.

While she was sure that Pearl's doctors here in Victoria were quite competent, there was a chance the doctors in Houston were better. And if she could afford the best doctors, why not use them?

Yes, it meant more time in Houston, more time away from her bakery and her home, more time with Grant, but that was inconsequential compared to Pearl's health. And the time away from Victoria would be much more bearable once Pearl was with her.

Though, to be honest, Pearl wasn't her only consideration. She had to think about the Cains too. They would back her up if she didn't want to move in with Cooper. But he would retaliate.

She looked down the block again. She'd lived here almost her whole life. Now life as she knew it was ending.

She stood. "I think I have to go to Houston. And I have to do what Grant wants."

"No," Cooper said. "You have options."

"I know, but he'll fight back. He'll go after Pearl and he'll go after the rest of you."

"We can take it."

"But you shouldn't have to." No, she would protect Pearl and she would protect the Cains. The only one she wouldn't be able to protect was herself. She would harden herself against him. She would barricade her heart. And if she ached every time he entered the room, well, she would just have to live with that. As long as she didn't let him close to her, she would be fine. Eventually. Someday. "This is my problem. I'll fix it."

Cooper nodded. "If you're sure."

"I am." Now she just had to pack.

Nine

Grant pulled up in front of the house less than an hour later, looking much calmer than he had when he'd left. Once again, Meg was sitting on the front step. This time, two suitcases sat beside her. She hadn't had much time to pack them and traveling with a toddler wasn't easy. At least, she didn't think it would be. The truth was, Pearl had never been more than twenty miles from home.

And now this.

It just seemed wrong to her. But she wasn't sure if that was because it felt so wrong for her or if it was wrong for Pearl.

Grant climbed out of the car and came around to lean against the passenger-side door. "Funny. I thought I made myself perfectly clear. Yet I don't see my daughter here."

Meg forced herself off the porch and down the path, her feet dragging as if she was walking through cake batter. And she had the feeling this was going to be just as messy.

She stopped a few feet away from him.

"Before I take you to her, I need you to hear me out."

His gaze narrowed suspiciously, but he nodded.

"This whole experience has been very weird for me," she admitted. "I spent my whole life knowing exactly who I was. Hollister's unwanted, bastard daughter. Then, two weeks ago, I find out that everyone has been looking for me. That I'm this 'missing heiress.' How can I be missing when I'm right where I've always been?"

Grant shrugged but didn't interrupt.

"Hollister wanted to find me, sure. But for all the wrong reasons. He wanted to find me because he wanted control. I don't want that for Pearl." She shook her head. "No. It's not even about what I want for her. I *can't* let that happen. Not to her. You have to understand. She has Down syndrome. She is beautiful and loving and strong-willed and delightful and funny. But in the end, she still has Down syndrome. Which means there might be times in her life when she can't make decisions for herself. Times when she needs someone else to step in and act on her behalf. If you're ever going to be a real father for her, then you have to have her best interests at heart. You can't do this partway. You can't be her father part-time. And you sure as hell can't do it as part of some power play against the Cains. You have to do this for her. Do you understand what that means?"

He nodded and for a second, she almost believed he really did. Almost. His gaze softened. For the briefest second, he looked like the guy she'd fallen for over two years ago. Tough, reserved, just a hint of vulnerability. That was a guy she could love. A guy who might love her back.

Part of her, the part that had fallen for him in the first place, wanted to stop talking now. To leave it where there might be some foundation that they could build a relationship on. Not a romantic relationship but a friendship maybe.

But she couldn't leave it at that. She couldn't just trust that what she wanted to see in his eyes was really there.

"Please, just think about this. Carefully," she practically begged. "Because once you're in, you're in. If you're doing this out of revenge, I'm begging you to walk away now."

Just like that. The kindness and understanding was gone.

His gaze hardened. "That's what you think? That I want my daughter out of revenge?"

"That's why you wanted me," she said softly.

Part of her wanted him to deny it. The rest of her knew he wouldn't.

He turned away from her, muttering a curse. Then a moment later, he turned back, his expression grim. "Yes. It's why I came after you to begin with. And then, at some point, I realized that what I was doing was no better than something Hollister would do. That's when I walked away. I'm not going to pretend that I wasn't an ass. But I stopped before I went too far."

"But you still want revenge on the Cains. And no matter how you slice this, if you hurt her, you'll hurt at least two Cains. Maybe more." Doubt flickered in his gaze and something in his expression softened. Maybe, just maybe, she'd made progress here. "Please. I'm asking you to reconsider. Even if you think you're doing this for the right reasons. Even if you think you know what you're getting into. You don't know. You can't know what it is to be a parent."

But she'd gone too far. She knew it the moment the words were out of her mouth. The lines of his face froze into disdain.

"You're right. I don't know what it means to be a parent. I don't know because you kept her from me. But that ends now. Go get my daughter."

"Grant—"

"I would never hurt her to get back at the Cains. And screw you for implying I would."

The raw pain in his voice was almost too much to bear.

"Okay then. Follow me." She nodded and turned to

walk away. Not toward her house but down the street to the house where Pearl was staying.

She felt Grant fall in line beside her. It sucked how aware of him she still was. How she could feel the zing in the air between them as he walked beside her. How the car-warmed scent of him still made her breath catch.

She walked faster, turning up the pathway to the red-brick house three down from hers. Janine opened the door before they even made it to the porch.

"Is she still doing fine?" Meg asked, as Janine opened the door wider, giving her a clear view of the living room, where Pearl sat in front of the TV in a tiny armchair.

One of Pearl's favorite shows was playing. On the TV an animated toddler tried to stand and walk while Vivaldi played in the background. Every time the cartoon baby fell on her bottom, Pearl squealed with delight, bopping up and down on her own bottom and clapping clumsily.

"She's just fine," Janine drawled. Then she looked Grant up and down, not bothering to hide her scorn. "Took you long enough. Then again, I never did think you were very smart."

But Grant seemed not to notice Janine at all. He didn't bother to greet her, even though she'd served his coffee nearly every day for months when he'd been dating Meg.

Instead, he pushed past Janine and Meg and walked into the small house. He didn't seem to notice the shabby decor or the worn carpet. Instead, he walked over to where Pearl sat watching television. He didn't say anything. He just slowly sat down beside her, facing her so that he could see both her and the TV at the same time.

And suddenly the man that he'd been for the past however many hours it had been since Cooper dropped the bomb on them—that angry, resentful man—faded away. The man she was afraid would use Pearl against her just vanished.

After a minute, Pearl—who was naturally so agreeable and open—glanced over and realized for the first time that someone was there beside her.

She looked up at Meg. "Mama?"

Meg knew she should say something here, but she couldn't get words past the lump in her throat. So she tried to smile reassuringly and nod.

Meg edged back into the shadows. Suddenly she wanted Grant to have this moment with Pearl all to himself. She didn't want to distract either of them.

But Pearl didn't look in her direction. Instead, she tilted her head to the side, considering this stranger and trying to decide if she was going to like him. Then she pushed herself up and toddled a step closer to the TV screen. She pointed at the ice-skating bear—the show was on to another segment now and another classical song played in the background. Then she clapped and laughed as the bear did a perfect triple lutz.

Grant tipped his head back and laughed, a low, wondrous chuckle.

Meg hadn't heard his laugh in more than two years and the sound of it carved her heart right out of her chest. The last time she'd heard him laugh at all, they'd been in bed together. She'd done something particularly naughty to him. There'd been whipped cream involved. His laugh was fun and sexy and incredibly tantalizing.

She missed it. She missed him. She missed the person she'd been when they'd been together. She missed the way he made her feel—the way he drove her body to distraction. The way he made her feel on the inside, too. As if she could do anything.

After a moment, Pearl stumbled back away from the TV so she could see better, but instead of sitting in her little chair, she sat down on Grant's lap. She stuck her fist into her mouth and gave a satisfied wiggle as she tucked herself against him. And just like that, Grant had won over another Lathem woman.

Then, just when Meg already felt overwhelmed, Grant tipped his head forward, his nose barely grazing the top of Pearl's hair. And he inhaled deeply.

Meg knew all too well what that was like. The scent of apple juice and Johnson's Baby Shampoo. The scent that flooded her with contentment and peace. Holding Pearl made her feel humble and as if she could climb mountains all at once.

Her heart pinged in her chest as she watched him sitting with Pearl, an expression of absolute awe on his face.

Meg turned away, squeezing her eyes shut as it hit her: Grant was going to be a good father.

He was going to fall hopelessly in love with Pearl, just as she had. He was going to coddle her and care for her and fight for her. All Meg's fears about him—all these fears, at least—were ungrounded.

He was going to be a good father.

That was what she wanted for Pearl, right?

After a healthy heart and long life, that should be the third wish. Another parent who would love her unconditionally. Another person out there in the world who would do anything for her.

As a mother, how could she not want that?

Yet, as a woman, it destroyed her. It left her with so many doubts.

What if she'd gone to him when she'd first realized she was pregnant? Her whole life might have been different. Pearl's life too. Pearl might have known the security of a loving father from birth.

Meg didn't harbor any fantasies that she and Grant would have gotten immediately back together. Her own heart had still been too raw. But at least there wouldn't have been this awful deception between them. The simmering resentment and anger. At least that would be different.

But however different things might have been, when she'd found out about Pearl, she'd been too angry to contact Grant. Too bitter.

Her mind rushed back over the past two days. Had there been a moment, at any point, when things might have gone differently? When she might have been able to broker some kind of peace between them? When she might have fixed this?

Maybe. But that moment had come and gone so quickly she'd missed it entirely. Now she was left with this tense truce. More of a cold war really. Each of them ready to trigger mutually assured destruction.

So this was what she could look forward to for the rest of her life.

Ten

Grant turned his car onto Highway 6, exhaustion pressing down on him. Despite how tired he was, he felt wide-awake, his mind buzzing as he passed the exit for Meg's motel. Just under twenty-four hours ago, he'd followed Meg's cab when it had gotten off at this exit. At the time, his only thought had been protecting her. Making sure she knew what she was getting into.

Now, his whole world had shifted.

The traffic was pretty light this time of night on a Sunday. He glanced into the rearview mirror. Pearl sat in her car seat in the back, her blond head tipped to the side as she slept. Beside her, Meg slept too, her head resting on the wing of Pearl's seat. She had spent the first hour and a half of the drive in the backseat with Pearl, singing to her. He'd now heard "Itsy Bitsy Spider" about five hundred times. Then, when Pearl had finally started acting sleepy, the song had shifted to a low and melodious version of "Somewhere Over the Rainbow."

Finally, Pearl had fallen asleep and Meg had drifted off just after. It had been a long day for all of them.

Completely alone with his thoughts, he tried to keep his mind on the road, but other distractions kept creeping in.

What exactly had he gotten himself into?

All day long, he'd been acting on instinct. He'd been moving forward, putting one foot in front of the other, trusting his gut to get him to the right place. Now, he wasn't so sure.

How could he block out the worried frown on Pearl's face as they'd packed so many of her belongings in the trunk of his car. The suspicion when they'd fastened her car seat in the back of an unfamiliar car. Suspicion that had turned to near hostility when Meg had coaxed her into the car seat. She'd calmed down when Meg climbed in after her and buckled herself in. Then it had been a fun game—having Mommy in the backseat with her. But that had lasted only about thirty minutes. Pearl had started crying. He'd felt as if he was having his heart ripped out of his chest, but he had no idea how to calm her tears. Hell, he wasn't even sure why she was crying.

Which brought him back to the question: What the hell was he doing here?

"You're having second thoughts."

His gaze jerked to Meg in the rearview mirror. She stretched a little, pushing her hair out of her face.

"I thought you were asleep," he said, careful to keep his tone soft so as not to wake Pearl.

"I'm a mom. We're like ninjas when it comes to power naps."

He still hadn't adjusted to the idea of Meg as a mom—forget as the mother of his child. He just couldn't even imagine her as maternal.

Sure, Meg had a nurturing quality to her—that went part and parcel with the baking. But she also had edge. Sass. She not only baked chocolate-chipotle cream pie, she'd licked it off his abs. She was hands down the sexiest woman he'd ever known.

Even after he'd left Victoria, she'd played a starring role in a good percentage of his fantasies. And now she was singing "Itsy Bitsy Spider." Which should have made her less appealing. That was how it was supposed to work, right?

But somehow, curiously, it didn't. That song, on repeat, lessened his anger.

Which was so not what he wanted right now.

She was stretching again. "How much longer?"

He glanced out the window, looking for landmarks. "Maybe twenty minutes." Of course, she wouldn't know this part of Houston. She wouldn't know where he lived. She'd never been to his house. He had a whole life she knew nothing about. And he was about to thrust her into it. He quashed a pang of guilt. "My house is in Montrose. Tomorrow morning, I'll have my PA arrange to have your car picked up from Portia's. And you'll need keys. To the house."

"Nice cover."

"What?"

"You *are* having second thoughts. You're nervous. So you're covering by managing the minutiae."

"I'm not having second thoughts."

"Oh, really?"

He'd lied to her too many times before to feel guilty about it now. Except he did. Probably because he knew she saw right through him.

"It's normal, you know," she said, stifling a yawn.

"What is?"

"The fear. The panic. The oh-holy-guacamole-what-have-I-gotten-myself-into. It's all part of being a parent. You'll get used to it."

He sat on that for a few minutes while he drove in silence. Somehow, her words soothed him. She seemed so good at this, it was hard to believe she ever had those moments. But maybe if she did, there was hope for him too.

She'd been quiet long enough. He wondered if she'd

fallen asleep again, but then she sighed, so he said, "You know, you could just let me stew in my own misery. You don't have to make me feel better."

"Yeah, I do," she said softly, her voice sounding wryly amused.

He nearly chuckled then. "You'd be hopeless in the banking world."

"Why?"

"Because we're adversaries. You're not supposed to be comforting me."

She sighed again, but this time, instead of sounding tired, she sounded sad. "Grant," she said quietly. "We're not adversaries anymore. We're going to be raising a daughter together. We're partners."

Meg barely noticed Grant's house when they arrived late on Sunday night. It had been such a long day. By the time she carried Pearl into one of the guest rooms that Grant had pointed her to, she was too wiped out to do much more than soothe Pearl back to sleep and then drift off herself. At home, Pearl slept in a crib in Meg's room, but she'd brought the Pack 'N Play from the bakery and that was where Pearl snoozed away now.

Now, in the morning light, Meg rolled over and looked around the room. She vaguely remembered how the rest of the house had the ornately feminine touches of a professional decorator, one who hadn't paid too much attention to her client's personal taste. This room, however, was more simply furnished. The furniture had clean modern lines. The woods were oiled rather than darkly stained. The fabrics were luxurious silks, tone-on-tone browns. The effect was soothing and warm but decidedly masculine. Not at all what the woman who had decorated the living room would have picked for a guest room.

Meg rolled over in the other direction and pushed herself

up. A Kindle sat on the bedside table next to a cell-phone charger. Again, not the pretentious stack of hardcovers a decorator would pick but a Kindle.

Frowning, Meg padded into the attached bathroom. Here, soothing greens complemented the browns. And again, there were the small personal signs that this was someone's bedroom, not a guest room—the partially used tub of shaving cream, the toothbrush, the medicine cabinet with actual medicine in it. She picked up a hairbrush and ran her thumb over the thick mound of bristles.

She unscrewed the lid of the shaving-cream tub and waved it under her nose. A woodsy scent with just a hint of citrus hit her. Yep. This was Grant's shaving set. This was Grant's bathroom. His bedroom. His bed.

Why had he put her in his bedroom?

Why did that bother her?

So what if she'd spent the night sleeping peacefully wrapped in the sheets that he'd slept in just a few nights before? So what if she'd rested her head where his normally did? So what?

There was nothing salacious about that. Nothing intimate.

She dressed quickly. Because she needed to feel more like herself, she put on her favorite Daisy Duke shorts and a fun crop top made out of vintage fabric. This was who she really was. The girl who made pies while singing along to the radio. Despite that she couldn't shake the feeling that Grant had invaded her. She went into the bathroom and brushed her teeth. It wasn't until she was brushing her hair that it hit her. She brought a single lock to her nose and sniffed. Great. She smelled like him. That's why it felt as if he was all around her. She'd slept in his bed and now she smelled like him. Like deliciously sexy man. Great.

She contemplated taking a shower, but all the soaps and shampoos smelled like him too. That would have to wait.

He was enough of a distraction when she hadn't actually bathed in him.

Instead, she dug around in her suitcase and pulled out the baby monitor she'd brought from home. She set it up near Pearl, clipped the receiver on her waistband and went in search of the kitchen.

Yes, she was a little freaked-out, but it was nothing some hot coffee and homemade biscuits couldn't solve.

While she was slinking through the froufrouey living room, she glimpsed Grant sitting at the table in the formal dining room with a plate of food and the newspaper in front of him. Rolling her eyes, she tiptoed past the door and headed for what she hoped was the kitchen. Who ate breakfast in the formal dining room? How douchey was that? How preten—

She pushed through the swing door into the kitchen and stopped cold. Grant's kitchen was sprawling and state-of-the-art, with acres of stone countertops, a sea of stainless-steel appliances and…a personal chef. And a maid.

"Oh," Meg muttered.

And there was the answer to her question. The kind of person who ate breakfast in their formal dining room…was a person with domestic help hanging out in the kitchen.

The two women, one a petite Latina wiping down the counters and the other a blonde with a chef's apron who had the look of a Russian model, both turned to look at her when she walked in.

The Latina blushed faintly, as though maybe they'd been talking about her before she came in, but the blonde woman just returned her gaze.

"Um…" Meg's mind went blank. Had she accidentally stumbled onto the set of *Downton Abbey*? She had zero experience with domestic help. Zero. Zip. Nada. "Um. Hi. I'm Meg."

She strode into the kitchen and held out her hand.

The blonde woman's lips turned down at the corners as if Meg was a sugar ant who'd sneaked in. Something unwanted to be smashed with her thumb and washed down the drain.

Finally she took Meg's hand and gave it a limp shake. "I am Grant's chef."

She mumbled a name afterward that sounded like Grendel. Meg didn't want to ask if she was really named after the monster from *Beowulf.*

The get-out-of-my-kitchen was implied.

"Okay." Meg turned to the second woman.

She wiped her hands off on a towel before shaking Meg's hand. "I'm Angela. Pleased to meet you. Can I get you coffee?"

"I can get my own coffee," she said hastily. Except when she looked around the room, the only thing that might be a coffeemaker also looked as if it had been stolen off the set of the latest *Star Trek* movie. "Um…if you could just…"

"I'm happy to get it for you," Angela said with a smile.

"Okay, then." She gave the kitchen another scan. It was so pristine it might have been professionally cleaned. Which, of course, it was. Her fingers practically twitched to bake something. Buttermilk biscuits with sawmill gravy. Chocolate, banana-pecan muffins. Fried doughnuts rolled in cinnamon sugar. Any of the above would work. All of the above would be better. But none of the above belonged in this perfect, pristine kitchen. "Maybe I'll just pour a bowel of cereal?"

Ms. Grump scowled. "I will make for you whatever you want."

"No, thanks." Meg smiled brightly. She owned a small-town bakery. Which meant she'd served more coffee and sweets to more surly people each week than most people encountered in a lifetime. She was not going to let Ms. Grump get her down. She slipped farther into the kitchen and stepped toward the pantry. "I can fend for myself. I'll just—"

"Would you like eggs?" Ms. Grump stepped in front of her, wielding a spatula as if it was a matador's cape. "Maybe an egg white omelet? Whole wheat toast?"

"No, thanks." Meg stepped to the other side of the chef. "I'll just poke around—"

Ms. Grump swung her spatula arm out in front of Meg like a traffic barricade. "I do not mind." She bit out every word as if it pained her to say them. "What would you like to eat?"

Meg sighed. Message received. This was Ms. Grump's kitchen and Meg was as welcome as E. coli. "What did Grant have for breakfast?"

"Mr. Sheppard has a spinach and egg white omelet with dry whole wheat toast each morning."

"Great." Geesh. No wonder he was so uptight. "I'll have that."

Meg spun on her heel and marched out of the kitchen. Once the door swung shut behind her, she leaned against the wall and sighed. Then she pulled the baby monitor receiver off the waistband of her shorts and brought it up to her ear. Past the static, she could hear the soft snuffling noises that Pearl made when she slept. "We're in a whole new world, bean. What are we doing here?"

Before she could come up with any satisfactory answers, she heard the shuffling of feet from the other side of the door. She sprang away from the wall just as Angela walked out carrying a tray with a cup of coffee, a sugar bowl and a tiny pitcher of cream.

"You can go on into the dining room, Meg. I'll bring the coffee in."

"Great." Guess that ruled out hiding in her room for the rest of the morning. Or rather, Grant's room.

She led the way into dining room, with Angela right

on her heels. Grant looked up only after Meg unclipped the baby monitor from her shorts and set it in the center of the table as she sat down.

"Good," Grant said brusquely. "I see you met Angela."

"Yep."

Angela hovered over her, moving items off the tray.

Meg wanted to run through her growing lists of concerns about staying here but didn't want to do it in front of Angela. Or was she supposed to just act as if Angela wasn't there?

Grant held up his coffee cup to the maid. "Would you mind getting me another?"

"No, sir."

"Also, when you're done in the kitchen, could you find a nanny service and arrange for them to send over some candidates for Meg to interview?"

And suddenly the issues of the room where Meg was staying and the pushy personal chef seemed minor. "I'm not hiring a nanny." She pinned Angela with a stare. "Don't call the nanny service."

"Of course you need a nanny," he said smoothly. "Angela—"

"No, I don't need a nanny. Pearl doesn't need a nanny."

Grant sighed. "Meg, be reasonable."

"I'm being very reasonable. I have only agreed to be here for a month. That's not enough time to warrant hiring a nanny. And during that time, I'm not going to be working. As far as I can see, the only benefit of being here in Houston for the next month is that I'll be able to spend all my time with Pearl."

Grant's gaze hardened. "I would have thought that the benefit of being in Houston was that Pearl would get a chance to spend time with me."

Meg sucked in a breath. Of course that was the point. Why did she have such a hard time with that? Did she subconsciously not want Pearl to get close to Grant? Or maybe even consciously? How could she ignore how much harder this would be on her if Pearl and Grant became close? How was she going to live the rest of her life with him forever right under her nose? How was she supposed to learn how not to want him?

"Yes," she made herself say. "Of course. Of course that's the point. But having a nanny here won't help you get to know her. Pearl doesn't let in just anyone. If there's a nanny here, caring for her all day long, she won't want another new person in the evening. She'll want me."

He considered this and finally nodded. "We'll see." Then he glanced over at Angela, who had been waiting by the door, her gaze darting from Meg to Grant through-out the conversation. "But I still want you to come up with a list of reputable nanny services, in case we change our minds."

Meg blew out a breath, feeling as if she'd won without really winning. Grant had agreed, but only for now.

Since they were already arguing, she asked, "When we got in last night, why did you put Pearl and I in your bedroom?"

He only considered the question for an instant before giving a disinterested shrug. "It was the logical place to put you. I'd seen how much stuff you have for Pearl. You'd said on the drive that you wanted to be in the same room with her. My bedroom is the biggest and is the only one on this floor. It made sense."

"Well, I'd rather be moved to another room. We can do it as soon as Pearl wakes up."

"None of the other rooms are big enough for her... what did you call it? Pack 'N Stay?"

"It's a Pack 'N Play. And I'll move some furniture around."

"Meg, that's not necessary."

"But—"

He pinned her with a stare. "What's really the problem here?"

She leapt up, suddenly too nervous to sit still. Too aware that they were essentially alone for the first time since they'd argued in the motel room. Too aware that the smell of him enveloped her every damn time she moved her head, because all of her hair smelled like him!

"I'm just not comfortable staying in your room, sleeping in your—" She paced the length of the dining room, pausing at the far end to glare at him. "Look, you want me to spell it out for you?"

Comprehension dawned on his face. He twisted slightly as he eased back, propping his elbow on the back of his chair, a slow smile spreading over his face. "Yeah, I kind of do."

Oh, this was too much! He was too arrogant. Too sexy. Too appealing. Worst of all, far too cognizant of his effect on her.

"Well, I'm not going to." Annoyed beyond belief, she started to storm out, but before she made it to the door, he was on his feet, blocking her way. She tried to dodge past him, but he used the move to cage her with one hand on the doorjamb and the other planted on the wall beside her head.

"Let me go," she muttered resentfully.

"I will." But he didn't move.

He stood there, looming over her. Invading her space, causing anticipation to dance along her nerve endings and heat to bloom in the secret places of her body. She may want to forget what it had been like between them, but her body remembered. Her skin remembered shivering with delight as he traced delicate paths over the most sensitive parts of her body. Her blood remembered throbbing as it pulsed through her clit. Her sex remembered clenching around him as a climax pulsed through her.

Finally, when he still didn't say anything, when the tension became too much for her, she forced herself to look up at him. Only then did he speak.

His hand slipped to her cheek as he gently brushed it with the back of his fingers. "You're not the only one this is hard on."

"I'm not?" She whispered the question.

"Damn, Meg, do you think I don't remember what it was like to be with you? Nothing else has even been like that. It was the best—" He cut himself off, his eyes dropping to her mouth, and for a second he seemed unable to even speak as his thumb tugged on her bottom lip.

Then in one rapid movement, he closed the distance between them, cupping her ass and lifting her up as he stepped between her legs. Trembling with need, she instinctively wrapped her legs around his waist. His mouth was on hers. His tongue in her mouth.

She didn't question. She didn't think. She only felt.

It was amazing. Everything she remembered. More. So much more that frantic need pulsed through her body and everywhere his hands touched she burst into flames. She was desperate and needy. His fingers hitched under her leg, caressing the skin bared by her shorts. She wiggled, and his fingers grazed her panties. She couldn't help it, she ripped her mouth from under his, tipping her head back to moan as his fingers slipped under her panties, teasing the moist flesh there before one of them plunged deep inside. Her breath came in frantic bursts as she tried to tamp down the scream of pleasure she felt burning inside of her.

She rubbed the apex of her legs against the hard ridge of his erection. It only took a second to find the rhythm she needed. With a few layers of clothes between them and his finger buried deep inside, she climaxed.

She wanted to do it again. And again with him inside her. And again with him in her mouth.

But some thread of reason returned. He straightened her clothes, and she managed, just barely, to get her legs under her when he lowered her feet to the ground. Then he pressed his forehead to hers, drawing in shaking ragged breaths as if he was as affected as she was.

She could have stood there in his arms all day... No, she could have locked the door to the room and spent the day in there doing a lot of things other than standing.

But a moment later, Angela bustled up, faltering outside the doorway when she saw them standing there. Grant straightened, giving Meg enough space to duck under his arm and away from him. Mortified, she practically ran to the other side of the table, feigning obsessive interest in the bit of yard outside the window while Grant sent Angela back to the kitchen. Now, all Meg could think about was whether or not what they'd done had been visible through those windows. Had any of his neighbors seen them?

The thought was sobering enough to bring Meg to her senses.

Whether or not anyone had seen them should have been the least of her worries. The most-of-her-worries should have been centered on how stupid she'd been to engage in some heavy petting with Grant at the friggin' breakfast table.

"Meg—" he started to say.

She whirled around to face him. "That can't ever happen again!"

She wanted to bolt, but before she could, he was there beside her, running a hand up her arm. Was that supposed to be soothing?

Shaking off his touch, she said, "You know I'm right. We can't do this kind of thing. If we're going to live together, we have to have boundaries."

She watched his expression as he considered her words.

"Meg, we're good together. You know that. You remember that as well as I do."

"Yeah. I do. But if that happens again, Pearl and I are moving out."

He studied her for a moment, looking as though he couldn't decide if he wanted to argue with her or just rip her clothes off. Finally, he nodded and then left the room without saying anything.

Which was for the best. She wasn't sure if she was up to resisting his arguments or him ripping her clothes off.

He was right. They were good together. The problem was, he was only talking about sex and for her their relationship had been so much than that.

Everything—every cell in her body, ever neuron in her brain, ever particle of her soul—remembered loving him. And remembered being ground into the dirt when he left.

Eleven

The next week passed in a blur for Meg. She never let herself think about what had happened between her and Grant in the dining room. Yes, he'd shaken her to her very core. Her need had shaken her. But she carefully locked those memories away in a tiny corner of her mind. She would deal with them later.

Besides, she had plenty to keep her busy in the meantime. She had multiple appointments with the lawyer Dalton had hired to represent her interests in custody matters with Grant. Though she liked the woman, who promised to make this as easy as possible on Meg, Meg still hated the idea of negotiating custody with Grant. She couldn't think too long about it, so she kept that part of her brain locked in stasis most of the time. Of course, the only thing she wanted to think about less was the idea of Pearl going under the knife. The appointments with doctors and surgeons seemed endless. That part of her brain she shut away too.

She knew what was in store for them with the surgery. She'd been researching it for a long time. She'd read so much of the literature about it, sometimes she thought she could do the surgery herself. Maybe in her sleep. After all, she did actually dream about it.

The procedure was a relatively simple one. The doctors would go in and sew a patch over the hole in Pearl's heart. As she healed the tissue of her heart would gradually grow over the patch. It would become a part of her. Forever.

And wasn't that what Meg feared most about Grant? He was in their lives now. Forever. Pearl's heart would grow around him and there would be no getting him out.

Meg knew this was a good thing. That Pearl deserved to have a loving father. Meg was worried about herself, because how was she supposed to function with Grant in their lives?

So, instead of asking herself those questions, she focused on Pearl's health.

She had feared that changing doctors and moving to Houston would slow down the timetable for Pearl's surgery, but the opposite was true. It turned out money really did move mountains. Or in this case, surgical schedules. And before she knew it, Pearl's procedure was on the books and only two weeks away.

Meg's anxiety over the impending operation diminished any pleasure she might have taken in being right about at least one thing: she truly didn't need a nanny. She had more than enough people spending time with Pearl as it was. Ms. Grump—whose name, it turned out, was Gisele and not Grendel at all— never warmed up to Pearl, but Pearl had Angela wrapped around her finger from the first smile. Grant went in to work late and came home early to spend time with her. Then, after her bedtime, he'd stay in his office late into the night finishing up the work he wasn't getting done during the day. Some days he didn't go in at all, but just spent several hours in his office on the second floor.

It seemed as if one member of the Cain family after another was at the house all the time. Laney brought her baby to play with Pearl one day. The next day Griffin and

Sydney came to meet her. Then Portia and Cooper came. Then Dalton and Laney came again.

By the time Monday rolled around—marking the end of her first week of living with Grant—and Sydney and Portia showed up on the doorstep, Meg finally made a joke about it.

"Okay," she said as she showed them into the living room, which had slowly been taken over by Pearl's toys. "I'm starting to think you don't trust Grant. Are you afraid he's going to murder me in the night?" As she said it, she reached down to pick up Pearl off her spot in front of the TV, but when she didn't hear the laughter she expected, she turned around to gape at Sydney and Portia. "I was joking. You know that, right?"

Portia's smile looked a little iffy. Her laughter a lot forced. "Sure. Of course."

Meg looked from one to the other. "You can't honestly think—"

"No, of course not." Sydney waved a dismissive hand. "Of course we don't think he'd hurt you. Physically. But the circumstances here are…unique."

"So you guys devised some sort of schedule to come and watch over me?"

"It's not a schedule," said Portia.

"Not formalized anyway," added Sydney. "Look, we want to watch out for you. There's nothing wrong with family looking out for family."

"Grant isn't going to hurt me. Or Pearl. I promise you that."

They exchanged worried glances, and Sydney said, "But he did threaten you to get you here. He did manipulate you. You don't want to be here. You're here only because he bullied you into it. You can't deny that."

"I'm not trying to deny that." So why did she feel so weirdly protective of him? But they didn't know what he was like with Pearl. Every time she tried to harden her heart against him, she'd catch him doing something incredible, like singing "Itsy Bitsy Spider" to Pearl, and her heart would melt all over again. "You have to try to see it from his point of view. He's missed out on eighteen months with his daughter. He's just trying to make up for lost time."

Did she really believe that? Or was she just making excuses for him? She didn't know anymore. Just a few days ago, she and Grant had been on opposite sides of this fight. So why was she defending him now?

Sydney and Portia looked as baffled by her lecture as she felt. "Okay," Sydney said slowly. "We'll back off. But you need us—"

"I don't need you to defend me! I've been on my own for a long time. I can take care of myself. Besides which, don't you think you're being at least a little bit rude? You're insulting him in his own home, in the presence of his child."

"We're looking out for family," Portia said gently. "And there are things about him that you don't know."

"What? That he blames Hollister for his father's death? That he hates the Cains? That he's publicly vowed to do anything in his power to destroy Hollister? Because I know all of that."

Portia frowned, looking genuinely concerned. "You may not know as much as you think you do."

"I know enough. I know he's the father of my child. That means I have to try to make peace with him. And I can't do that if I'm always expecting him to screw me over."

"You're our family," Sydney said again, with the kind of ferocity that made Meg wonder what her story was.

"Well, he's the father of my child. That makes him *my* family. And yours, too, for that matter." Neither Sydney nor Portia looked ready to accept this fact. So, after a moment of excruciating silence, Meg added, "Now, if you'll excuse me, it's nearly time for Pearl's nap. I trust you can see yourselves out."

With that, she plucked Pearl up and turned her back on her sisters-in-law. She went into the kitchen, and, ignoring Ms. Grump's glare, handed Pearl to Angela, who took her off to the bedroom for a new diaper while Meg poured Pearl a sippy cup of milk. Her hands were shaking as she returned the milk to the fridge. She just stood there for a moment, staring at the sippy cup, her hands propped on her hips to hide their tremor and her head ducked to collect her thoughts.

God, she hoped she wasn't making a mistake. She had so few friends in Houston and absolutely no family—anywhere. She'd either just isolated herself or begun to broker peace between the Cains and Grant.

Of course, standing here freaking out wouldn't quell her fears. So she screwed the cap onto the sippy cup and took Pearl from Angela. Meg figured that she and her daughter could both use a little *Goodnight Moon* and a nap.

But when she left the kitchen for the master suite where she and Pearl were still sleeping, she had a clear view of the second-floor balcony that overlooked the living room and the foyer. And there was Grant, standing with his elbows propped on the railing, looking quite comfortable and rather pensive. When she stopped short, his gaze met hers.

"How long have you been standing there?"

"Long enough to hear you defend me."

She nodded, not knowing what to say. She hadn't even been aware that today was one of the days he was working from home. She hadn't meant for him to hear that, but she wasn't sure why it bothered her that he had. Maybe because it made her too vulnerable. Despite what she'd said to Portia and Sydney, she didn't trust him. Family or not.

She knew better than anyone that a family connection didn't guarantee affection.

So she pulled Pearl closer and glared at him. "Don't make a liar out of me."

"I don't intend to."

She nodded and crossed the living room, suddenly excruciatingly aware of his gaze on her back. She heard him walking down the stairs but ignored the sound until he reached for her arm. Turning, she held Pearl between them like a shield and tried to ignore the sizzle that spread over her arm where his fingers touched her skin.

"Thank you," he said simply.

"You're welcome." And then she added, just in case it hadn't clear the first time, "If you prove me wrong, I'll go all *Fried Green Tomatoes* on your ass."

He looked at her blankly. "I don't know what that means."

"It's a movie about a woman who owns a restaurant and kills her jerk of a husband and then disposes of his body by making big vats of chili."

Amusement dawned in his gaze. "Ah. I see."

"Just don't forget I own a restaurant too."

"Yeah." He smiled broadly. "But you make primarily fruit-based pies. I'm not worried."

"I could get creative." But somehow, this conversation that she'd meant to sound threatening, was sounding much more like flirty banter.

Exactly the same kind of flirty banter that had landed him in her bed to begin with. Maybe he sensed it too, or maybe she just imagined the heat simmering in his gaze.

Before she could scurry away to safety, he said, "Tell me something, Meg."

"Um, okay."

"Why'd you sell the bungalow?"

The question was such a change in topic it took her a moment to process it. "I don't know," she lied.

"But you grew up in that house." When she didn't say anything, he added, "Your mother grew up in that house."

"The time was right for the market."

"You grandfather lived his whole life in that house."

"Yes." She didn't need him telling her how important that house should have been to her. She knew. It had been everything to her. It had been her last connection to her grandfather. Before Grant, she'd lived her entire life there.

But she'd also had her heart broken in that house. She'd been betrayed in that house. She'd lost her faith in humanity in that house. She'd lost her faith in herself.

She didn't even like to think about that house, but she was glad he'd brought it up. It was just the reminder she needed. Flirty was the last thing she should be doing with Grant. Well, second to last, after making out in the dining room.

She turned to leave, but only made it a few steps away before he added, "By the way, you were right about not needing a nanny."

She turned and looked at him, trying to judge if he was being serious or just messing with her. He certainly seemed serious, so she nodded. "I'm glad you think so, because tomorrow afternoon, I need you to watch her for a couple of hours."

"Why?"

"Because I got a call from Dalton this morning. Hollister is back in town. My brothers are taking me to meet him tomorrow."

Grant arrived at the Cain mansion thirty minutes prior to when Meg said she was going to show up. Yeah, he knew she didn't expect him, but he would deal with the repercussions of that when he had to. He was going on pure gut instinct here.

Not that his gut was doing him any favors these days. After all, it had been instinct that had made him kiss Meg that first morning she'd been in his house. He'd kissed her because he hadn't been able to stop himself. Because he hadn't had the strength to walk away.

Even though she'd participated in the kiss, even though she'd obviously enjoyed his touch, ultimately it had driven her away. Ever since then, she'd made a point of not being alone with him. So following his gut had gotten him jack.

Not that he even knew exactly *what* he wanted.

All he knew was that he wanted Meg safe. And he didn't trust the Cains not to put their own needs well before hers.

So he sat outside the house in his Lexus, waiting for Meg to arrive. When her Chevy rattled around the corner, he climbed out of his car. She must have noticed him as soon as she drove up because she didn't walk up to the house but walked straight over to his car.

She arched an eyebrow. "I thought you were going to be back at the house, immersed in *Sesame Street*."

"Good guess, but I thought I was needed here."

"And our daughter is—?"

"With Angela, who was delighted to have the excuse to skip cleaning and play with Pearl."

"Oh, I bet. But you know, I could have asked her to do that. If I'd wanted you here."

"You're about to meet your father for the first time. The sociopathic father who screwed over your entire family and then abandoned you."

"Hmm…the last time we were discussing him, you called him a psychopath. Has he been downgraded?"

"My point is, I don't trust him alone with you."

"He's in his midseventies and from what I've heard, an inch from death. I don't think he's a threat."

"I'm not worried about him beating you. Hollister was never the type to resort to physical violence. I don't want him getting in your head."

"I can handle myself. Besides, my brothers will be there."

As if on cue, the front door to the Cain mansion opened and Dalton came out to stand on the front stoop, glaring at them where they stood on the street.

She glanced from her brother and then to him, looking exasperated. "I think we're causing a scene. You can come in, but please try to restrain yourself."

"I'll behave if he does."

She eyed him again, as if trying to figure out whether she could trust him. Then she turned and started up the path, muttering under her breath, "If Hollister is in a pissy mood, I hardly think having the son of his sworn enemy hurl insults at him will improve matters."

Still, there was something reassuring about the weight of Grant's palm at her back as she walked up the steps. Through the fabric of her shirt, he traced tiny circles with his hand. The movement was intimate, but felt supportive rather than erotic. It soothed her enough that she blew out a low slow breath.

Dalton eyed Grant with suspicion when they reached the door. "Hollister isn't going to like this," he muttered.

Again, she felt weirdly protective of Grant, even though he was a big boy and could take care of himself. So she inched closer to Grant before saying, "Hollister can just deal. He can't deny I'm his daughter, we've made sure of that. He might as well find out now that Grant and I have a relationship." The word *relationship* made her cheeks burn, because it implied more than was strictly true, but neither Dalton nor Grant called her on it, so she continued. "I figure, let's go in with guns blazing. There's no other way to do this."

Neither of them argued with her.

In had been nearly five years since Grant had seen Hollister in person. Though ostensibly they moved in the same social circles, Grant made a point of avoiding venomous snakes. Steering clear of Hollister had become much easier since Hollister had handed over the reins of Cain Enterprises to Dalton. In that time, Hollister's health had been on the decline. He'd had several major heart attacks and at least one serious stroke. Personally, Grant thought Hollister was too damn mean to die and would probably outlive them all.

At least, Grant thought that until the moment Hollister's nurse wheeled him into the living room where they'd all been waiting. Dalton, Griffin and Cooper were all there, as well as Grant and Meg. All five of them stood when the nurse rolled Hollister in. Grant stayed in the far back corner, where he was unlikely to attract Hollister's notice. Grant wasn't sure what Meg had expected, but when she saw her father for the first time, she sucked in a breath, either out of surprise or to brace herself, Grant wasn't sure which.

Hollister, once a tall, barrel-chested man, had shrunk to a mummified version of his former self, as if a mere touch might snap his desiccated bones and blow his flesh to dust.

Delicate oxygen tubes crossed under his nose to hook behind his ears. A colostomy bag hung from the back of his chair. He brought with him the smell of decay.

For some people, old age brought kindness and understanding, a desire to make peace with the world and the past before they met their maker. For Hollister, it had brought only frustration and resentment. He had once been a giant among men. He had once controlled fortunes and lives. Age had reduced him to this. Grant almost felt sorry for the man.

Then Hollister looked Meg up and down and huffed.

"These papers here—" he clutched several sheets of paper and waved them weakly as he drew in a shuddering breath "—seem to say you're my daughter." He clenched his fist, crumpling the pages before tossing them on the ground. "But I won't believe it until I've taken a look at you myself. Come here."

Meg marched forward, chin held high. She stopped a few feet in front of him but said nothing.

He gestured for her to come closer. "Get down here where I can take a proper look at you." Then he turned and barked at the nurse. "Hilda!"

The nurse must have known just what he wanted because she scurried across the living room and returned with an ottoman, which she sat on the floor just to the left of the rests that held Hollister's feet.

He jerked his hand toward the ottoman. "Sit." Then he barked at Hilda again. "Bring a light. It's too damn dark in this house. Caro never did know how to light a room."

Caro hadn't lived in this house for more than a year, but based on the elegant and tasteful decor, he'd say Hollister hadn't changed a thing about it.

Hilda rushed out of the room and returned a moment later with a swing-arm lamp that she set up behind the ottoman. Meg sat down on the edge of the ottoman, her shoulders stiff, her head held high.

Hollister leaned forward, looking her over. Twice he reached out a trembling hand and nudged her chin this way and that. Grant wouldn't have been surprised if the old bastard asked Meg to bare her teeth for him.

Finally he sat back with a huff. "Well, you have the Cain eyes, that's for sure, but you have your mother's look about you."

"I'm surprised you remember my mother," Meg said with a bite in her voice.

Hollister's gaze narrowed. He opened his mouth to speak but was overcome by a fit of coughing. Hilda rushed forward with a wad of tissues, which Hollister brought to his mouth. When he was done, he tossed them back at her, covered in bright red blood. Hilda must have seen that coming, because she'd whipped out a pair of latex gloves and put them on. Now she collected the tissues and, ignoring the few drops of blood on her scrubs, deposited the whole mess into a red biohazard canister on the back of Hollister's chair. The whole thing was done with such efficiency, Grant had no doubt this was a common occurrence. Maybe this time, Hollister really was on his deathbed. Coughing up blood implied blood in his lungs, which could be indicative of any one of nasty health issues.

After a moment of wheezy breathing, Hollister spoke again. "Yes. I remember your mother. She never told me about you." He eyed her again. "Dalton tells me you have a kid."

"I do."

"And she's sickly."

"She has a heart problem and needs surgery."

"Humph." Hollister pinned her with his gaze. "You drink too much while you were pregnant?"

Grant automatically took a step forward, but Cooper grabbed his arm, not to stop him necessarily, but to give Meg a chance to fend for herself.

Meg met her father's gaze directly. "No. I didn't." Her tone was as steely as his had been. "It's a congenital birth defect. No amount of excellent prenatal care can change genetics."

Hollister looked around the room then and seemed to see Grant for the first time. "Is that the father?"

Meg glanced at him. "Yes."

Hollister wheezed, his thin lips twisting into a skeletal smile. "And who are you?"

It was a clever tactic, pretending not to recognize a known enemy as a way of controlling the negotiations, but Grant wasn't about to fall for it. The gleam in Hollister's gaze was too malicious for this to be anything other than deliberate.

"I'm Grant Shepard, CEO of Sheppard Bank and Trust."

"Ah. Russell's boy. That defect in the genes probably comes from you then. Russell always was weak."

Cooper grabbed his arm again, but this time, Grant wasn't going anywhere. Hollister could insult him or even his father all he wanted. Grant wasn't going to take that particular bait.

"You get him to marry you?" Hollister asked Meg.

Before she could answer, Grant said, "We're engaged." Everyone, including Meg, turned to look at him. He added, "She agreed just last night. We weren't planning on telling anyone yet. But since you asked…"

The lie seemed to satisfy Dalton, Griffin and Hollister, but Cooper looked suspicious. And Meg looked downright flummoxed.

"I don't know how I feel about my grandkid being a Sheppard." Hollister frowned and poked a trembling hand in Meg's direction. "You should keep the Cain name when you're married. That way, this kid of yours can be a Cain."

Well, Grant would say this for Hollister's arrogance: it made everyone else in the room look better. Meg seemed to forget Grant's lie and instead focused on her father.

"When I marry—" She shot Grant a look. The *if* was heavily implied. Okay, clearly she hadn't completely forgotten. "—I will be keeping my own name. Lathem."

Hollister made another harrumphing sound. "Tell me, are you as worthless and mewling as she was or do you take after me?"

Meg's chin bumped up a notch. "I like to think I take after my grandfather. The man who raised me."

Hollister's eyebrows shot up. "He was a clever old bastard. Yes. That'll do." Then he looked over at his sons. "So, which one of you gets Cain Enterprises? Who found her?"

"I did," Griffin said quickly.

Grant jerked his head around to look at Griffin, but no

one else moved. No one else was as shocked by this pronouncement as he was. Which meant they'd planned this out ahead of time. Of course, Griffin hadn't found her. She'd presented herself to them. But they were probably worried that Hollister might change the deal if he knew the truth. He was a crazy old bastard and he loved nothing more than having his kids dance on his strings.

Hollister nodded. "Well then, boy. Cain Enterprises is yours." He coughed again. He and Hilda repeated the elaborate bloody-tissue dance. Then, when that was over, he gave his nurse a nod. As she started to wheel him away, he said, "I'll have my lawyers draw up the papers to hand the company over to you."

Dalton stepped forward, waving a hand to stop Hilda. "If you don't mind, we've already taken care of it." As if on cue, a trio of men in business suits emerged from a back hallway. Grant recognized them as the senior partners of one of the more prestigious law firms in town. "Buckner, Handley and Roch already have the paperwork all drawn up. They've handled your personal legal work for twenty-five years, so you know you can trust them. All you have to do is sign the paperwork, then Handley here will notarize it. Your new will will be filed and held and you never have to think about it again."

Hollister's gaze went suddenly hard. "Don't rush me. I need to think about it."

"There's nothing to think about. We have—" Dalton seemed to catch himself. "Griffin has met the stipulations of the previous will. He found your missing daughter. The tests prove she shares genes with all three of us, so she must be your child. And she's obviously convinced you. All you need to do is sign the papers."

Hollister considered for a moment. In that moment, Grant knew in his gut that Hollister would never sign the papers. He would never legally acknowledge Meg as his daughter. To do so would mean letting go of the last strands of control he held over his family. All his life, they'd danced to his tune. Especially in the past few years, with this quest he set them on. Yes, on some level, he had wanted to find his missing daughter, but mostly, Grant now realized, he'd wanted to control his sons. They had been drifting further and further away from him, driven away, actually, by his manipulative bullshit. This quest had been his way of drawing them back to his side. He would never be willing to give that up.

Maybe this should have relieved Grant. After all, his own plans had hinged on Cain Enterprises' continued instability. The longer Hollister put off signing the papers, the better. Better yet, if he died without ever signing them, his estate would be held up in legal battles for years, increasing the chances that Grant would eventually gain control over enough shares to take over the company entirely. This moment should be a dream come true.

But there was Meg to think of and for her, this may well be a nightmare. She claimed she didn't want the money, but she needed the independence it would give her. To hold her own in this family, her pride demanded that she have money of her own.

Moreover, she needed the closure. Not for anyone else, but for herself. Half of Houston had already accepted her as Hollister's daughter. The longer he waited to acknowledge her, the harder it would be on her.

And on Cain Enterprises, for that matter, because Hollister would seem more and more senile and ineffective.

And that's when it hit Grant. The real reason the Cains had introduced Meg to society at the Children's Hope Foundation gala.

But before he could say anything else, Meg raised a hand to get everyone's attention. "I'd like a moment alone with Hollister."

Everyone just stared at her, and then everyone—even Hilda—protested. But Meg remained firm.

"Just a few minutes will do." To Hilda she added, "I won't upset him. I promise."

But Grant saw the gleam in her eyes. She might have promised not to upset Hollister, but she definitely had an ace up her sleeve.

Finally, Hollister nodded and a few minutes later, they all went into the living room while Meg wheeled Hollister into the back room for their few minutes alone.

Grant waited until Dalton had picked a spot on the sofa and then he went and sat next to him. "Making Hollister appear incompetent was always part of the plan, wasn't it? It's the real reason you introduced Meg to everyone at the gala."

Dalton gave him a shrewd look. "This isn't something I want to discuss with a competitor who already owns nine percent of the company. If Meg wants you here for support, I'll respect that. I won't ever trust you and I won't stop trying to convince her the truth about you, but I will respect that. But—"

Griffin stepped in, stopping Dalton's rant with a hand on his shoulder. "I think what Dalton is trying to say is stick to family matters and stay away from the business."

And wasn't that interesting. The Cains knew that he'd been buying up stock. They didn't know how much, since he'd bought an additional seven percent through a shell company. Still, he was on their radar. Curious to see how much they really knew, he baited them a bit. "On the other hand, it's a family business and I *am* family now."

"Yeah. I might be more inclined to believe that if Meg hadn't looked like she wanted to strangle you when you said it."

Grant shrugged. "We have a tempestuous relationship."

"All the more reason for me not to discuss Cain Enter-

prises business with you. Besides, I'm not the CEO anymore. Griffin is."

"Fair enough, but the way I see it, you're laying some
pretty tricky groundwork. If Hollister doesn't fall in line,
you're going to have him declared incompetent. You'll
divvy up his estate yourselves. But that's a dangerous
game. While the case is tied up in court—and make no
mistake, he will take it to court—Cain Enterprises stock
will plummet. You'll be vulnerable."

"Which should thrill you," Dalton said wryly.

"Maybe."

But it wouldn't thrill Meg, he was sure of that.

"You know, that's some pretty manipulative crap."
Grant didn't know whether to be impressed or horrified.
"Even for a Cain that's pretty bloodthirsty."

"You think we're doing this just for the money?" Dalton asked. "I guarantee you, we're not. We're doing this
for the company. Hollister is unstable. If he keeps this up,
we're not the only ones who will suffer. Every Cain Enterprises employee and customer will too. This plan isn't
ideal, but it's the best we've got."

Would Meg agree to go along with it or would she think
the price too high?

She seemed to have no love lost for her father, but was
she really ready to have him declared senile? Didn't that
seem harsh? Grant, on the other hand, had been watching
Hollister for years. He had no compunction at all about
breaking Hollister's spirit. But Meg would. Sweet, loving Meg. She would want to do the right thing. She would
second-guess herself.

Or would she?

After all, it was Meg who was talking to Hollister right
now. It was Meg who had seemed to predict this turn of
events and had devised some sort of contingency plan.
Was it possible that Meg was one step ahead of them all?

That was the moment Grant knew he was in serious trouble. Here, in this family of cutthroat ambition and ruthless conniving, Meg could hold her own. She was smart enough and determined enough that she would never let anyone take advantage of her.

If Meg had been a sheep in a family of wolves, it would be easy to pat her on the head and dismiss her. But that's not who she was. At all.

She was a wolf herself. A wolf in vintage print and cherry bomb lipstick, but still a wolf. She was tough and sassy and stubborn and she could hold her own against almost anyone.

How had he let himself forget that, even for a moment? Maybe the bigger question was, how could he not love that about her?

Twelve

Meg had heard stories about Hollister all her life, first from her mother, then from her grandfather. Even from the people in Victoria who were old enough to remember him from the few months he'd lived there when her mother had fallen in love with him.

Other kids she'd known had been afraid of the monster in their closet. Or of the dark. Of thunderstorms or rattlesnakes. Or ghosts.

Not her. She'd been afraid of Hollister. The monster under her bed had been her father.

But that was a long time ago. She'd gotten over her fear of her father the same way humans had gotten over their medieval fears. She'd brought him out into the light. She'd researched him, learning everything she could about who he was and what he'd done to her family and why. Nearly thirty years ago now, he'd come to Victoria to purchase software that her grandfather had developed. It was the early eighties. Geologists were just beginning to use computers to aid in oil exploration. Her grandfather's software—which had originally been designed to search for aquifers—was revolutionary, but he'd refused to sell it to Cain Enterprises. So Hollister had seduced Meg's mother and had her steal the software for him. And Meg had proof.

Alone with her father, for the first time in her life, she stared him down. He wasn't that scary, after all. He was as mean as dirt, but he wasn't scary.

She wheeled him into the room and shut the door behind her. If the shelves lining the walls were any indication, this room had once been a library or maybe an office, but it had been converted into a bedroom. A hospital bed jutted from the far wall, flanked on either side by medical equipment. This was undoubtedly where her father would live out his final days.

She positioned him by a wingback leather chair beside the bed. Then she sat down herself because maybe, just maybe, meeting him on a level playing field might help.

"Well," Hollister barked. "If you dragged me in here, you must have something you want to say."

Hmm. Her father. Quite the charmer.

"I do," she admitted. "I think you should sign the papers." Except she'd phrased that wrong. She was too used to cajoling customers and Hollister wouldn't respond well to that. "You need to sign the papers."

Hollister waved a hand. "I will. Eventually. Probably."

"No. You need to sign them now."

"I—"

"No," she said again, more forcefully this time. "Finish this. You and I both know you don't have time to waste."

"You know nothing," he scoffed.

"I know coughing up blood is a very bad sign. You wanted me here. I'm here. You want to live out the last of your days surrounded by family, your family is here. Maybe you even wanted to see which of your sons was most ambitious or most loyal. Well, now you've seen. Now finish it."

Hollister leaned forward. "You think you can boss me around, missy?" His chest heaved, but he didn't cough, and so she didn't hand him a tissue. Instead, a few speckles of blood sprayed onto his lips. "Well, you can't. I'm twice as tough as you and five times as stubborn."

"I don't think I can boss you around." She pulled a sheaf of papers from her purse and handed them to Hollister. "I know I can." She gave him a good minute to look them over. To get the full scope of what he was seeing. When his fingers began to twitch, as if he wanted to tear the papers to shreds, she added, "Of course, these are only copies. I have multiple copies of the originals. Both here in Houston and in other locations. Nowhere you'd be able to find them."

He thrust the papers back at her. "What do you want?"

"I want an end to this. I want only what you promised. You swore you would give your entire estate to whichever one of your sons found me. Griffin did. So sign over the estate to him. Do it today, or you will be hearing from my lawyer. And my lawyer will not be from a firm you've been dealing with for years. My lawyer will be *my* lawyer. He'll make the case that much of Cain Enterprises' profits for the past twenty-five years are based on the software you stole from my grandfather. Software I have the patent to."

"If it goes to court, it won't win." He began to cough in earnest now. His lips were bright red with it.

"Maybe not. But the case will be tied up in court for years. Maybe decades. And while it is, the company you sacrificed everything for will wither and die." She stood then and started for the door.

"You're doing this for him, aren't you? Because he thinks he'll be able to swoop in and buy up stock. Take over the company. It's what he's always wanted—" Hollister started coughing again.

Meg handed him a wad of tissues and he held them to his mouth, but somehow he still managed to get just a few drops of blood on the papers. That was fitting. There always had been blood on them.

Meg stood, tapping the clean edge of the documents against her palm. "Shall I leave these here?"

He shook his head, tissues still held to his mouth.

"I trust we're done here?"

He glared at her. "He's using you. You're just too stupid to see it."

"I'll send in the lawyers with the paperwork for you to sign."

She wiped the papers off with a tissue and then tucked them back into her purse before fetching a trash can and holding it out so Hollister could throw away the bloody tissues. She didn't bother with the latex gloves. She would definitely be washing her hands on her way out.

Grant paced the living room, wanting Meg to be done talking to her father. Actually, Grant, Dalton and Cooper all paced the living room. Only Griffin—the brother who seemingly had the most at stake—appeared relaxed. He sat on the sofa, checking his email on his phone. Hilda hovered near the door, ready to go to Hollister if he needed her.

The three lawyers, each clutching a briefcase, stood off to the side. If any of this struck them as weird—and how could it not?—they didn't say anything. They must have been versed in the Cain family history, because no one protested. No one seemed concerned that they might be treating Hollister unfairly, which seemed like a reasonable concern. If Grant didn't know what was going on, if he didn't know Hollister, he would be worried. When a dying man's four children all got together to bully him into signing a new will, it didn't look good. But the lawyers obviously understood that this was what Hollister had agreed to.

As for Grant, he wasn't the least bit worried about Hollister. Meg, on the other hand…

She was strong enough to handle anything Hollister

dished out. Grant knew that. And yet…and yet, he knew what an asshole Hollister could be. And it killed Grant knowing she was in there with him alone. Meg obviously thought she was prepared to deal with Hollister on her own, but she wasn't. Not really. Even if she could handle this situation, there would be emotional aftereffects for a long time.

Then, just when Grant was ready to storm the gates and rescue Meg, the door opened and she strolled out. She crossed straight to the lawyers.

"He's ready to sign the papers now. You can go right in."

They nodded, disappearing into the room after Hilda.

Meg turned around and smiled grimly at her brothers. "Honestly, I don't know how you put up with him for so many years." Then she frowned slightly. "Or how you all turned into seemingly decent human beings. How is that possible?"

Dalton nodded as if he agreed. "I've been lucky."

"I'm just too stubborn," Griffin said with his normal charming smile.

Cooper shrugged. "Don't look at me. I grew up two thousand miles away from his toxicity."

Meg just nodded, as if that all made sense. Then she turned to Grant. "Let's get out of here."

But he crossed his arms over his chest, putting himself between her and the door. "So that's it?"

She frowned. "What's it?"

"So you convinced Hollister to sign the papers."

"Yes. I did."

"The papers that are going to hand over Hollister's entire estate to Griffin?" She frowned, as if she wasn't sure what point he was trying to make, but Grant continued, "He's not the one who found you. He didn't earn that money."

"Technically, none of us *earned* it."

"That's your inheritance. And you're just handing it over to Griffin."

"I told you all along I never wanted the money."

Before he could say anything else, Griffin stepped between them. "Look, this is what we—what all four of us—agreed to. The best way to ensure the stability of the company was for me to claim to have found her. It's just easier that way. Once everything is transferred over to me, I'm going to divvy it up among the four of us. It'll take some time, but that's the plan."

Griffin flashed one of his smooth aren't-I-trustworthy smiles.

Yeah, Grant didn't trust him for a minute. "A lot could happen in the time it takes to get this all sorted out."

Griffin's smile took on a hard edge. "Such as?"

"You could easily change your mind about exactly how much you think your siblings deserve. For that matter, you could simply misplace some of Hollister's assets."

"That's not going to happen."

"It better not, because—"

But Meg stepped between them and put her hand on his chest. "Grant." She waited until he looked at her. "It's not your problem."

"But—"

She shook her head. "I'm leaving now. And you should probably come with me because something tells me you won't be welcome here after I'm gone. Especially with you acting like such an asshole."

"Well, she definitely has the Cain intelligence," Cooper said wryly.

Grant looked around the room. Yeah, Meg's brothers didn't look exactly thrilled with him right now. Go figure.

When she turned to leave, he followed her out to the car. He waited until she'd beeped her car unlocked before saying, "Look, I'm sorry. I just don't want them taking advantage of you."

"Sure, I get it." She swung the car door open and climbed inside. "I'm the ignorant small-town girl. Easy to take advantage of. I can see why you'd be particularly concerned about my gullibility."

"That's not what I meant." He braced one hand on the door and the other on the frame so he could lean down into the vehicle "I just think you're not concerned enough. You don't know what they're capable of."

"You're right. But here's the deal. I don't particularly care. I don't care about any of this. You know what I do care about? The fact that my baby girl is going under the knife in less than a week. She's having open-heart surgery. It's a big deal and it scares the piss out of me. That's what I care about right now. All the rest of this stuff, with Hollister and the millions, even your silly, out-of-the-blue pronouncement that we're engaged, it's just background noise to me."

And just like that, he felt like a total ass. Because, of course, what she said was true. Pearl's surgery was a big deal. And it had totally consumed his thoughts. Except he really was worried about Meg. Maybe he shouldn't be. Maybe he didn't need to be.

But he knew the kinds of things the Cains were capable of. He knew because he was capable of the same things.

Thirteen

The next week passed so quickly Meg hardly had time to blink. She would have thought, after the way Hollister had loomed over her life for so long, that finally meeting her father would have rocked her foundations. That she would suffer from the aftershocks for weeks to come.

But instead, just as she'd told Grant, all her energy was focused on Pearl and before she knew it, all the pre-op appointments had passed and it was the night before Pearl's surgery. Long after the little girl was asleep, when Meg was still awake, she pulled on some yoga pants and a tank and crept through the house to the kitchen. In the few weeks she'd lived here, she'd given up cooking for herself. Ms. Grumpy Gisele guarded the kitchen like a harpy. The one time Meg had made herself a midnight snack, Ms. Grump had actually confronted her the next day with the skillet Meg had used, claiming Meg hadn't done a good job washing it.

So, she'd given up. She'd let Ms. Grump boss her around and she'd stayed out of the kitchen. But she'd been baking all her life and there were some problems only cookies could solve. Which was why, at eleven o'clock, she'd clipped the baby monitor to her hip and crept into the kitchen. For a long time, she simply stood in the pantry, surveying the ingredients. Then she went to the fridge and did the same. And then the freezer. Finally, she pulled several plastic tubs from the pantry and went to turn on the stove. Tonight she was baking, even if she had to pay the price tomorrow.

Grant woke up in the guest room with a crick in his neck—because damn it—he'd fallen asleep sitting up with his laptop open in front of him. But after several minutes of lying in bed, he realized it wasn't only his discomfort that had woken him up. It was the smell of something burning. He sat bolt upright, his finger practically already dialing 911.

But before he could pound out the three digits, he remembered: Meg was here. And Meg baked in the night.

Then he inhaled a deep breath and was hit with the scent of something nutty. Something indulgent but homey. Something unlike anything he'd ever smelled, certainly unlike anything he normally encountered in his house.

He pulled on a pair of shorts and stumbled downstairs. Not because he was hungry. Not because he remembered so clearly—God, as if it had been seared onto his retinas—that tiny, white-trimmed black nightie that Meg used to bake in. Or the way she'd flitted around the kitchen in her house, looking like a cross between a pinup girl and a French maid. He got hard just thinking about it.

No, that wasn't why he was going downstairs either.

He was checking on potential fire hazards. That was all. That was it.

You smelled something baking in the middle of the night. You went and checked on it. After all, the houses in this part of town were all well over fifty years old. And, yeah, he'd had the kitchen remodeled when he bought the place last year, but faulty wiring could have caused the oven to turn on in the middle of the night. And for all he knew, Gisele had stored something flammable in the oven. He was not sneaking down to spy on Meg. He was being safe. That was all.

Besides, it was his house. He had every right to go downstairs. No matter what time of night. Maybe especially at night.

Of course, when he came downstairs, his house didn't look anything like his house anymore. Sometime in the last two weeks, it had been transformed into…something else. All the various knickknacks the decorator had picked out had been boxed up and put into storage. Or, if he was lucky, into a donation drop box somewhere. He had never liked what the decorator had done; it was a cautionary lesson in the power of the words *Do whatever you think best*.

Because he'd never liked the style in the living room, he'd spent most of his time in the master bedroom, the only room he had cared enough about to voice an opinion on. So his house had always looked unlived in.

Now, the opposite was true, even at night when everything was silent, instead of ringing with the sound of Pearl's cheerful, *Mama's* and *no, no, no, no, no, no, no's*. All the ornamentation had been stripped bare and replaced with brightly colored kids' toys. Puzzles and picture books had replaced the tchotchkes and pretentious coffee-table books. All the electrical outlets were covered. The hard edges of the coffee table and fireplace hearth had been wrapped in foam. Scuff marks marred the wooden floor where little feet had pushed a toy car along. This wasn't his house anymore. Maybe it should have bothered him, but it didn't. Not when it kept Pearl safe. Not when it meant he had her in his life. Because what was the alternative? No Pearl, with her sweet smile and sparkly eyes? No cute toddler dancing in front of the TV? No Meg?

That just didn't work for him.

From the kitchen came the whirring of a motor—maybe

the mixer? He sidestepped a stack of blocks and walked through the swing door into the kitchen, only to stop cold. What the...?

The counters—all of them—were covered with cookies. Trays and plates of them. Racks of them. Pans of them. And there in the middle was Meg.

She had moved the mixer—which usually sat unused in a corner—onto the island and was now standing beside it watching the contents of the bowl. Her back was to him. She was dressed in black yoga pants and an orange tank top. Her feet were bare. Her hair—with its chunky streaks—was up in a ponytail high on the back of her head. Not all of her hair was long enough to fit in the ponytail, so she had a fringe of a few inches along the back of her neck, a delicate wisp of hair in her natural light brown.

There was something so vulnerable about finding her standing barefoot in his kitchen, late at night. Something intimate.

After a minute, she flicked off the mixer and scraped down the side of the bowl, something he'd watched her do countless times before. There was a lot of scraping in baking. A lot of putting things back where they belonged.

In that lull between mixes, he asked, "What's all this?"

She jumped, turning to face him, wielding her spatula like a sword. Then she pressed her free hand to her chest and blew out a breath. "You scared me."

Yeah, well, she scared him too. Her strength and vulnerability. Her fearless love. Her delicate beauty. He had no defenses against her and it terrified him.

"So what is all this?" he asked again.

"I'm baking." She looked at the countertop stretching out in either direction and seemed almost surprised by what she saw. Clutching the spatula in both hands, she added, "Cookies."

"All of them?" he asked, because he'd never seen so many cookies in one place since…well, probably never.

"Over here we have cranberry oatmeal," she said, using her spatula like a pointer. "And beyond that is chocolate shortbread. There are peanut butter cookies over here. And nut rolls on the other side."

"That's a lot of cookies."

She tilted her head slightly and said, "I couldn't decide what to make. You have a very well-stocked pantry but no chocolate chips. What's up with that?"

He gave the acres of cookies another quick survey, before glancing at the clock on the microwave. "You've made roughly twelve dozen cookies and it's 1:20 in the morning. But the fact that I don't have chocolate chips in my pantry is the strange thing here?" Emotion flickered across her face. A mix of panic and irritation. As if she knew she was being irrational but resented the fact that he'd called her on it. Gently, he said, "Come on, Meg. It's time to go to bed."

As if she didn't even hear him, she turned her attention back to the mixer and flicked it on again. "No. I just finished toasting the flour for the next batch of shortbread."

He took a step closer to her, putting a hand on her shoulder. Her muscles were as taut as the stone countertops, her tension almost palpable. He reached past her to turn off the mixer. "Enough."

She turned it back on. "I'm almost done."

"Come on, Meg. I know you. You bake because you love it. You bake when you're happy. You bake when you're content. But when you bake like this, it's because something is wrong."

She whirled to face him, her eyes snapping and sharp. "Yeah. Impressive deduction skills. My daughter is having open-heart surgery tomorrow. I'm stressed. Somebody give this guy a pipe and deerstalker hat."

"You're not doing anyone any favors." He turned the

mixer off again. "In a couple of hours, when you have to go wake Pearl up to head to the hospital, you think she's not going to notice that you're exhausted and frazzled? You think she's going to be calm if you're freaking out?"

"I think my only chance of not freaking out tomorrow is to freak out now if I have to. So stop being so damn judgey-judgey and leave my mixer alone, damn it." She flicked the mixer on again and this time stood right in front of it, her fingers wrapped around the switch as if she was ready to fight him over it.

"I'm not judging you." He wrapped his fingers around hers, urging her to look at him, but she kept her gaze steadfastly in front of her.

"Of course you are," she snapped. "You have no idea what I'm going through."

"What? You think a father can't worry like a mother?"

"You've been her father for a matter of weeks. You can't know what it really means to be a parent. You haven't gotten up in the middle of the night to feed her and change her diaper. You haven't held her when she got her shots and stroked her hair when she was sick. You haven't stressed out over doctors appointments or cried when you were exhausted and couldn't get the car seat in. That's what it means to be a parent. Come back to me when you've done all those things."

She moved to walk past him, but he grabbed her arm. "Yeah. I've missed out on a hell of a lot because you've kept my daughter from me. It would be better for both of us if you stop throwing it in my face."

Regret flickered across her features and she looked as if she wanted to say something. Maybe apologize again. Then she shook her head and said, "You can't imagine—"

"Like hell I can't. You think I'm not worried? You think I'm not terrified? Why the hell do you think I wanted the surgery done here? In Houston, where we have some of the best doctors in the world? Why do you think I—?"

This time, she was the one who switched off the mixer. She turned, her eyes flashing as she waved a spatula inches from his nose. "This isn't about you. It has nothing to do with you. Don't you dare try to make this yours."

She might as well have punched him. "This *is* mine," he said more fiercely than he intended. Until this moment, he hadn't realized he felt that way. Yes, he'd been saying it all along. She was his daughter. But he hadn't felt it until this moment. "This fear and worry? It is just as much mine as it's yours."

"Bullshit," she said fiercely, but the tears in her eyes nearly broke his heart. "If it goes badly tomorrow, I lose everything."

"You think I don't? If something happens to Pearl, I don't just lose a daughter, I lose the only chance I'll have to get to know her. If this goes badly, I will never get to stroke her hair when she's sick. I'll never get to put that car seat in so you don't have to stress out over it. And I'll never get to stay up all night trying to get her to sleep." He grabbed both Meg's arms then, not because she was trying to walk away this time but because that thought shook him so badly he needed something to hold on to. "That's why I'm not going to let that happen," he said fiercely. "I promise you. She is going to be okay."

He couldn't think when she looked up at him like that— with that mixture of sympathy and hope. As if he wasn't the enemy. As if he wasn't the asshole who'd screwed her over and broken her heart. He couldn't think and he couldn't stand it, either, because there was just a hint of faith in her gaze. As if she believed him when he said Pearl was going to be okay.

Of course, the truth was, he had no idea if it would be okay. He'd made her a promise he had no way of keeping.

Which just slayed him. His little girl's life would be on the line tomorrow and there wasn't anything he personally could do to keep her safe. He had no way of protecting her tomorrow during surgery. No way of protecting Meg from the heartbreak she'd face if something did go wrong.

That was the thought he'd been quashing all day. The panic that threatened to chase him down and beat him senseless. The fear that would eat him alive if he let it.

Instead of staring it down, he did the only thing he could think of to keep it at bay. He pulled Meg into his arms. To his surprise, she let him.

"It'll be okay, Meg," he said again. "I promise it'll be okay." *Please, dear God, let it be okay,* he prayed silently.

For a moment, she stood stiffly, and then leaned into him and clamped her arms around his waist. Breathing a sigh of relief, he settled his arms against her back. She burrowed her face against his chest.

He'd forgotten this—how well she fit against him, with the crown of her head tucked under his chin. Either forgotten it or buried it too deeply in his memory. She fit against him like no other woman. She fit against him as if their bodies had been engineered for one another.

Indeed, maybe they had. It felt like that sometimes. As if she'd been designed to torment him. To bring about his downfall. To absolutely destroy him.

No matter how good she felt in his arms, it was torture, because holding her only served to remind him of how it had been between them.

Since that first morning at breakfast, they'd both been avoiding this, dancing around one another so they wouldn't have to touch. Wouldn't have to face the memories of how good they'd been together. Her arms tightened around him and he could feel the spots where each of her fingers pressed against his back.

She sank against him, flattening her cheek to his chest.

She drew in a shuddering breath and he felt a faint dampness seep through his shirt from the tears she hadn't shed when they were fighting. Something deep in his chest tightened in response.

That's when he knew. He'd been kidding himself.

Yes, he'd wanted Meg and Pearl to move in because the doctors in Houston were better. And yes, he'd done it so he could get to know Pearl. And yes, he wanted it to be easy on them all. But it wasn't just that. No, when it came to Meg, things were never simple. They were never obvious.

It wasn't just about Pearl. It wasn't even about his anger or his wounded ego. It was about Meg.

It was about his need to have her close. To just be near her. To have another shot—and maybe this time he wouldn't screw it up.

He felt a momentary burst of panic. Because this was not how it was supposed to be. He was supposed to be in control. What was the point of working so ruthlessly to put up defenses against her if they crumbled the first time she looked up at him with tears in those mesmerizing blue eyes of hers?

Awareness danced along his nerve endings. They were alone, something he'd studiously avoided since the morning after she and Pearl had moved in. He'd carefully kept layers of people between them. Yet here they were, all alone. In the middle of the night. Desire curled its way through him, replacing all the fear and tension that had been devouring him all night. It was a want that went deeper than mere physical desire.

He didn't just want to sleep with her, he wanted to consume her. To devour her. To sear his brand on her very soul so that she'd never again doubt she was his. He wanted to possess her.

And he knew she felt it too. She had to.

He took a long, shuddering breath, and then another, struggling to regain his control.

Slowly, he brought his palm to cup her cheek. He brushed his fingertips across the contours of her face, forcing himself to keep the touch light as he tucked her hair behind her ear. His fingers lingered there, on the spot where her neck and jaw merged. He felt her pulse as it thundered through her.

The feel of her luscious skin made his mouth go dry. He swallowed before dipping his head and bringing his lips to hers. He heard a quick intake of breath and then he was aware of nothing except how she felt in his arms. Warm and welcome. Like heaven itself. Like bliss.

She rose up on her toes to meet him, her silken lips opening beneath his, her hot little tongue darting into his mouth. He groaned, slipping his hands down to cup her ass as he pulled her fully against him and lifted her up to sit on the counter.

Her fingers dived into his hair, urging him to deepen the kiss. He plunged his tongue deeper into her mouth, wanting to drink up all of her, needing to explore all the honey-sweetened corners of her.

Her mouth wasn't enough. He slipped his lips lower to her neck. To the shell of her ear. To the pulse point at her collarbone.

He wanted to consume her. To be consumed by her.

"This isn't a good idea," she muttered.

He pulled back enough to look at her through desire-hazed eyes. "No. It isn't."

He waited, pulse pounding, but she didn't say anything else, and he couldn't resist kissing her again. He slipped a hand up under her tank top to skim along the silken skin of her ribs, which seemed to shudder under his touch. He palmed her breast, even as he kissed his way down her neck to nuzzle her tank down to expose her nipple, which peaked with desire. He kissed her there, swirling his tongue over the tender flesh and sucking it deep into his mouth. She arched against his arm at her back, groaning as he massaged her breast. He simply couldn't get enough of her. She smelled like spice and vanilla and tasted like honeyed regret and lost dreams.

She gasped as he moved on to the other breast.

"This is a horrible idea," she said breathlessly. "This solves nothing."

He pulled back and looked at her again. "I know." She was tempting beyond reason, but if she asked him… "Do you want me to stop?"

"No." She slipped her thumbs under the waist of her yoga pants and shimmied out of them.

She tossed them aside, leaving herself bare from the waist down, her tank top shoved up, one breast naked, her folds moist with her desire. She was absolutely irresistible.

He knelt before her, spreading her thighs with his hands before slipping his thumbs up to part her glistening sex. Her bud seemed to throb against his tongue as he sucked it into his mouth, giving it the same attention he'd given her breast. He thrust his thumbs into her as she arched and bucked against him. She felt like heaven and hell all rolled into one as she came against his mouth.

When he stood up, she tightened her legs around his waist, pulling him against her. She kissed him even as she reached for the waistband of his shorts, shoving them down.

She buried her face against his neck, nipping at his skin.

"This doesn't mean I don't hate you," she said fiercely.

"I know." It broke his heart, but he did know that.

"I just need…"

"I know."

"It wasn't enough." She palmed his erection, stroking it with eager fingers.

"I know."

A moment later, she guided him into her, pulling his hips hard against the apex of her thighs.

And he did know. Even as he lost himself in the heated bliss of her body, he knew. It wasn't enough. It wouldn't ever be enough. Small scraps of her would never be enough. He wanted all of her, body and soul, and damn it, that's what he would have.

Fourteen

Meg woke up well before five, alone in the huge bed in the master bedroom. Pearl slept peacefully in the Pack 'N Play in the corner. Grant was nowhere to be found, though Meg was almost certain that he had slept beside her for some small portion of the night.

However, she refused to think about that. About Grant or about what they'd done the night before or even about what it might mean for their relationship. Instead, she dressed quickly and quietly and went out to start the coffee. She doubted she'd be able to choke down any food, but coffee was always essential.

She expected to find the kitchen a wreck, which was how they'd left it the previous night. Instead, the counters had been cleared off. Ms. Grump was at the sink, scrubbing dishes. On the counter sat two travel mugs of coffee. One was black, just the way Grant drank his. The other lightened to the pale mocha that Meg preferred. Between the two mugs sat an insulated tote bag stuffed with snacks, chilled bottles of water and carefully packaged cookies. Meg stared at the interior of the bag, trying to dislodge the lump in her throat. Obviously, Ms. Grump had done this. The gesture was so kind, so unexpected, it could mean only one of two things. Either Pearl had finally wormed her way into Ms. Grump's affections or pity had softened Ms. Grump's heart. Meg chose to believe it was the former. This was one of those times when she simply had to be optimistic. Pessimism was too crushing.

Besides, she'd done all her indulging in despair last night and it had opened her up to a whole host of trouble. She wasn't going down that path again.

Grateful, she took a sip of her coffee and, before heading back to the bedroom to wake Pearl, simply said, "Thank you."

Ms. Grump didn't turn around but stilled for a moment before nodding and mumbling a cool "You're welcome."

Back in the bedroom, Meg changed quickly into clothes that were functional and comfortable, a pair of worn jeans and a T-shirt bearing the Hogwarts crest with the words *Still waiting for my letter*, emblazoned underneath. Today was a day she needed to believe in magic.

As prepared as she'd thought she was, a thousand tiny things cut at her. First was the groggy way Pearl made the *more* sign as Grant buckled her into the car seat. It was the sign Pearl made when she was hungry. "Mama!" she pleaded, making the *more* sign again and again.

"Sorry, honey," Meg murmured. "Afterward, okay?"

Pearl frowned, and made the sign again and again. Once he'd climbed into the driver's seat, Grant took Meg's hand and gave it a squeeze. She met his gaze for the first time that morning—because she hadn't been ready to face the question she might see there. "There's never been a time when she's ever asked for food and I haven't been able to give it to her," she said softly.

"I know," he said, pulling out of the driveway.

In the back, Pearl made the *more* sign again, ripping another chunk out of Meg's heart. What would it be like to be a parent who routinely couldn't feed her hungry child?

"You going to be okay?" Grant asked.

"Yeah." Despite her fears, there were worse things than heart surgery.

Even this early, there was traffic in Houston, but Grant's house was close to the hospital, so it was only a matter of minutes before they pulled into the parking lot. Pearl, cheerful despite her hunger, smiled as they went into the hospital, instantly winning over the nursing staff, who let Meg and Grant stay with Pearl in the prep room, holding her hand until she fell asleep.

As Pearl's hand slipped out of Meg's, she felt Grant's hand on her shoulder. She looked up to see the nurse hovering nearby, clearly ready to usher them out.

"It's time," Grant said.

"I know." Still, as Meg gently laid Pearl's hand down on her chest, her own heart twisted, because no matter how unlikely it was, she couldn't shake the fear that this was the last time she'd see her baby girl alive. Despite the emotional turmoil of the previous night, despite their fight, despite the anger she'd been so stubbornly clinging to, having Grant by her side gave her the strength to stand and walk away from Pearl.

At the door, the nurse gave a smile that managed to be both solemn and encouraging. "I'll finish prepping her here and then bring her into surgery. I'll be with her the entire time," she said, repeating all the information Meg and Grant had been given in the pre-op appointment. "It's not a long surgery, but don't be surprised if it's several hours before the doctor comes out to see you. But don't worry, we'll come get you before she wakes up. She'll never even know you were gone."

The nurse gave another reassuring smile. Quite simply, this was her job. What she did every day. Somehow, knowing that did help.

Still, Meg might not have actually drummed up the strength to leave the room if it hadn't been for the steady pressure of Grant's hand at her waist. As they made their way down the hall, Meg was only vaguely aware of shuffling her bags from one shoulder to the other. Suddenly she was exhausted. Still nervous, still dreading the coming hours, but just bone weary.

So much so that when they walked into the waiting room, it took her a moment to realize that Grant had stopped by the door. Frowning, she turned back to look at him. He tucked his hands in his pockets and arched a sardonic eyebrow, nodding in the direction of the waiting room.

She turned back and then blinked in surprise. Yes, she'd noticed that there were other people there, but that was hardly surprising, since this was a busy hospital. What was surprising was that most of the people were here for Pearl. Dalton and Laney, Griffin and Sydney, and Cooper and Portia. They'd all come. And for the first time in her life, Meg felt as if she had a family she could depend on.

The hours seemed to stretch endlessly. People kept offering her tea. She kept drinking it, only to be offered more, as if tea was the great panacea. Even though she was happy to have her family around her, at some point she stopped noticing the other people in the room. So when an older, well-dressed blonde woman came in, Meg didn't even look at her. Until Grant stood and crossed to give the woman a hug. And then Griffin did the same. And then Dalton.

Meg was more than confused. Most times these men were in the same room together, it seemed as if it was all they could do to keep from punching one another. So who was this woman they were all so apparently fond of?

Meg shook off her nerves and walked over to where the four of them stood. Grant immediately introduced her. "Meg, this is Sharlene Sheppard. My stepmom."

Meg's manners overcame her confusion. She held out her hand. "It's lovely to meet you."

But Sharlene ignored her extended hand and instead wrapped her in a tight hug. "Don't be silly, my dear. You are the mother of my grandchild. Which makes us far too closely related to shake hands."

"Oh," Meg managed to gasp out before the air was squeezed from her lungs. And then when she was finally released, she shot Grant a confused look. "Grandmother?"

Sure, she had read somewhere that Grant's father had remarried after his mother's death, but she'd assumed he wasn't close to the woman since Grant hadn't mentioned her once in the time Meg had been living with him.

As if to answer Meg's unspoken question, Sharlene pulled back and held Meg at arm's length to study her. "So, you're Meg."

"I am."

Grant spoke up. "Meg is—"

But before he could finish the sentence, Sharlene reached out and gave him a slap on the head that was equal parts playful and peeved. She turned to him with a raised eyebrow. "Now, are you going to explain to me why you didn't call me and tell me about Pearl's surgery?" Then she clucked her tongue disapprovingly. "For that matter, why didn't you call and tell me about Pearl?"

Grant shrugged. "When you left for the ashram, you told me you didn't want to hear from me unless it was an emergency."

"I meant an emergency about work. Last time I took a vacation, you called me three times about bank business. I would have thought it was understood that if some long-lost relative showed up needing surgery you would have known to call."

Sharlene was obviously equal parts Southern charm, protective mama-bear and force-to-be-reckoned-with. None of which made deciphering these relationships any easier.

While Grant talked to Sharlene, Meg quietly slipped back to her seat, her concern about Pearl briefly eclipsed by Sharlene's entrance. After a few minutes, Portia came and sat beside her. "You look confused."

"I think I am."

"By Sharlene?"

"By the fact that she seems almost as close to Dalton and Griffin as she does to Grant."

At this, Portia gave a quiet little laugh. "Yes. I suppose it is odd, isn't it?" Then she gave Meg a studied look. "Do you know the history of Sheppard Cain?"

"I know there's bad blood between the families."

"Oh, I didn't mean the history of the families. I meant the history of the company. Though, I suppose it's really the same thing."

"The company?"

Portia took a sip of her tea, seeming to consider her words for a moment. "Back in the seventies, back when Hollister and Russell Sheppard were business partners, together they owned Sheppard Cain. Sheppard Cain focused on banking and real estate development, but they dabbled in oil exploration too. Sharlene was Hollister's personal assistant as well as his mistress. It all went south in the mid-eighties, probably about the time you were born. They had a falling-out. They split the company. Sharlene must have been tired of the way Hollister jerked her around because she left him and went to work for Russell. Or maybe she left Hollister for Russell and then the company split, I'm not sure. Eventually, they got married. When the company split, Russell Sheppard got the banking branch. Hollister got the real estate development as well as the seemingly worthless oil investments. Which, it turned out, weren't worthless at all. Right after the split, Cain Enterprises released the computer software that changed the face of oil exploration. There are a lot of things that probably no one but Sharlene and Hollister know the timing on. Did she leave him for Russell before or after the split? Did he screw his former partner out of billions out of greed or revenge? No one but Hollister knows. But due to the timing, he had to have known what the oil investments were worth. He turned Cain Enterprises into the billion-dollar company it is today."

"Sheppard Bank and Trust is no slouch," Meg said, feeling strangely defensive. And also strangely invested in the story. Somehow hearing the tale helped distract Meg.

"True. Grant has the heart of a ruthless pirate. But when the company was run by his father...well, Russell lacked the killer instinct. And he was never the same after being screwed over by the man he thought was his best friend."

Meg thought about all the history Portia had just recapped and could only shake her head. "It is weird though."

"Why?"

She looked at Portia, arching her eyebrows. "Oh, the fact that Grant and the Cains hate one another. And have for most of their lives. But then Grant's stepmother—the one he's superclose to, apparently—is like family with them." She paused, raising her eyebrows, and then added slowly, "Because she was their father's mistress. Before she married his father." She gave a shrug. "I'm just saying. It seems weirdly...I don't know, incestuous or something."

"Because she was with Hollister and with Russell?"

"Yeah."

"Let's just say, you'd be hard pressed to find a beautiful blonde woman in Houston Hollister didn't sleep with. Your mother wasn't the only one he screwed over."

"I never thought she was."

Of course, Meg had known about the bad blood between the Sheppards and the Cains, but hearing it spelled out like this...it was both worse than she'd expected and more tawdry all at the same time. It seemed silly almost, in the context of what she was going through today. Her daughter was in surgery. Everything seemed petty and insignificant in comparison to that. It seemed absurd that Hollister and Russell's twenty-five-year-old feud still affected so many people.

But no matter how absurd it seemed, she felt the ripple effect of the feud as strongly as anyone. Because that oil exploration software—the product that had put Cain Enterprises on the map in the oil business and made them billions—that software had been developed by her grandfather.

A part-time geologist, a full-time hippie and a groundbreaking programmer, her grandfather had developed that software—long before she'd been born—for the simple reason that he'd wanted to make the world a better place and had believed freeing up natural resources was the key. When he'd refused to sell it to Hollister, Hollister had played dirty. He'd seduced her mother. He'd tricked her into betraying her own father. When he couldn't buy the software outright, she'd stolen it for him and destroyed the evidence that her father had created the software.

Hollister hadn't just stolen from Meg's grandfather, he'd destroyed the entire family. No one needed to convince Meg that Hollister was evil.

All her life, she'd resented not just her father but her mother, as well.

It was her mother who'd been weak and gullible. Her mother who'd fallen for Hollister. Who'd given him that kind of power.

But now she had to wonder. Had she done the same thing with Grant? Hadn't she too fallen for a charming, rich, manipulative man? Was she any less vulnerable and gullible than her mother had been? Was she repeating her mother's mistakes?

For her own sake and Pearl's, she hoped not.

Fifteen

Somehow, having Sharlene there only made Grant feel more like an outsider. Even though Sharlene was the closest thing he had to a mother, in some weird way, she belonged as much to the Cains as she did to him. Much as Meg did. It was impossible for him not to resent their presence when what he really wanted to do was be alone with Meg. That was his daughter in the operating room. Their daughter. Was it so wrong that he wanted to be the one to comfort Meg?

But instead, Meg was deep in conversation with Portia, and Sharlene was talking to Griffin and Sydney. Feeling too worried to sit still, Grant headed down to the cafeteria in search of a decent cup of coffee, and on the way back took a detour at the serenity garden near the waiting room.

Which was where Sharlene found him nearly a half hour later.

He glanced over at her as she walked in. The garden was located in an open-air atrium. He guessed the hospital was going for a Zen feel, because there was a koi pond with a trickling stream. A wooden footbridge crossed the stream. That's where he stood, his elbows propped on the railing.

"Let me guess," he said. "It was Grace who spilled the beans."

"Of course it was. You know your sister can't keep a secret. She would have been here but Quinn has some nasty virus that Grace didn't want to spread around." She stopped beside him on the footbridge and together they stared out at the fish circling the pond. "Though why you thought you had to keep it a secret from me, I'll never know. Unless—" she gave him a sharp look "—you're planning on shipping Pearl and Meg back to Victoria after the surgery and never seeing them again. Are you?"

"Of course not. For someone who only got back last night, you sure seem to know a lot about Pearl and Meg."

She shrugged. "Like I said, Grace can't keep a secret."

"How much did Grace tell you?"

"Enough."

"Enough for what?" he asked, dread layering itself over the nerves he already felt about Pearl's surgery. This was the real reason he hadn't told Sharlene about Meg and Pearl. Sharlene was one of the few people he really valued. She wouldn't approve of what he'd done.

"Enough to know that Meg must have been part of some scheme you worked up to get revenge on Hollister. Enough to figure out that you probably regret what you did." She sighed, turning to face him. "I worry about you, Grant."

Yeah. He knew that. "Because I'm as much of an asshole as Hollister."

She shot him a look, frowning. "Because you've spent so much of your life resenting him. You've been so angry. For so long. You've blamed him for everything that was wrong in your life. Your father's life. My life."

"If I blame him, it's because he caused so much misery." He turned to look at her now. "You can't deny it. He made you miserable."

"Ah, honey." Sharlene reached up to cup his jaw. "No one makes us miserable unless we let them."

"I don't believe that. Some people are such bastards,

they make everyone else around them suffer just to be spiteful."

"And is that the kind of man you want to be? A bastard like Hollister?"

"All I ever wanted was for him to pay for what he did."

"But it's not your job to make him pay. Don't you see? You said it yourself. He's the bastard. He's already paid." She turned and looked back out at the stream and the pond. "Your father and I never had Hollister's vast fortune. Your father's heart gave out and we didn't have as long together as I wanted, but the years we had together were happy. The years I've had with you and your sister have been happy too. And personally, I think nothing infuriated Hollister more than seeing other people happy. I think it would drive him crazy to see you and his daughter happy together."

With that, Sharlene turned to leave. He watched her go in silence.

At the door back into the hospital corridor, she slanted him a sly glance. "That is, if you think she could make you happy."

Of course, for him that wasn't the question. With Meg and Pearl, he'd been happier than he'd ever been in his life. Whether or not he could make them happy was the real question.

After a while, Meg began to realize Grant had disappeared. At first she just assumed he'd stepped out for moment, but the minutes ticked by and he didn't return. She checked the time on her phone, flipped through a magazine. Sipped some tea. Checked the time again.

Where had he gone?

Surely he wasn't out in the hall taking business calls.

Surely he hadn't left.

Not that she expected him to sit by her side all day, holding her hand, but last night he had seemed as wrapped up in this as she was.

She checked the time again. Hours had passed since they'd left Pearl. So where was Grant?

Meg stood, but before she could take a step, Sydney was by her side.

"Do you need something? You need fresh tea?"

"No, I…" She looked around the room. There was another family ensconced in a second cluster of chairs and sofas, but other than that, the Cains were everywhere. Was this why Grant had made himself scarce? "I'm fine," she said quickly. "I just want to stretch my legs."

A few minutes later, she found Grant in the hospital's courtyard meditation garden.

He was sitting on a bench beside a gurgling fountain, his elbows propped on his knees.

He looked up when she walked out into the garden, but he didn't stand.

She leaned back against the closed door and said, "You never struck me as the type who'd be intimidated by a roomful of Cains."

His lips twisted into a faint smile. "Not intimidated so much as…outnumbered."

When she crossed the small courtyard to his side, he scooted over, making room for her on the bench.

"I may be outnumbered, but I don't mind the solitude. You don't have to wait out here with me."

"I know." She lowered herself to the bench, hesitated for only an instant before sliding over next to him. His arm fell naturally to her shoulder and it felt good there. Right.

The Cain support meant the world to her. For so much of her life, she'd been alone. The only child. The motherless child. The orphan. The single mom.

Now, for the first time, she had a big extended family. It was both wonderful and a bit overwhelming. But in the end, no matter how great her brothers and their wives were, she alone was Pearl's mother.

But Grant was the girl's father and despite the things Meg had said last night, she did believe he loved Pearl.

She allowed her head to drop to his shoulder, allowed herself the moments of quiet comfort. Still—as always— she felt the buzz of awareness just under the surface. As always, it was scary how aware she was of him. Just the simplest touch had her nerves buzzing. But today felt different too. Calmer, maybe. As if it was easier to just be with him.

Then he said the one thing she never expected to hear from him.

"I think we should get married."

She stilled, for a moment not even daring to breathe. Then, slowly, she extricated herself from under his arm and cleared her throat. "Married?"

"I want us to be a real family. I want us to live together."

"Here in Houston," she said, just guessing.

He nodded, with only a hint of a frown. "Of course."

"I can't leave Victoria," she said a bit numbly. That was just an excuse, but it was a good one, so she clung to it. "I can't leave the bakery."

"You've left the bakery for weeks now and things have been fine."

"There's a difference between finding someone to look after the shop for a couple of weeks and moving permanently to a city three hours away."

He shrugged. "We'll find a way to make it work."

"Why?" She twisted on the bench and looked at him. "Why should I turn my life upside down? Why should you? Why not just let us go back to the way things were?"

"She's my daughter."

"That's not a real reason. There are millions of men—

probably hundreds of millions—who father children every day and don't give them a second thought."

"Hundreds of millions? Every day?" he asked wryly. "That's a bit of an exaggeration, don't you think?"

She rolled her eyes in annoyance. "The precise numbers aren't my point."

"I know."

"Most men don't care how many kids they father. Mine didn't."

"Exactly," he said, his voice suddenly harsh. "Your father didn't. Look, I know what Hollister did to your mother. To your whole family. He abused the trust of an innocent woman for financial gain. And I—"

But he broke off, as if he couldn't say the words aloud. The anguish there pulled at her. "And you nearly did the same thing to me," she finished for him.

"Not the same thing. But close enough."

She nodded, finally understanding. "So you feel like this is your only chance at redemption. That if you become a part of Pearl's life, if you're a real father to her, then maybe you're not as bad as Hollister."

He looked surprised by her words, as if he hadn't considered something so obvious to her. He wasn't a bad man. Not by a long shot. He'd just gone off course.

"Grant—" she began.

But before she could say more than that, he cut her off. "I'm not the only one with something to gain here," he said. "Here in Houston, Pearl would have access to the best of everything. The best health care. The best occupational therapists."

"Yes, but—"

"And you won't have to worry about the money."

"The money?" she asked cautiously.

"Your inheritance from Hollister. All that money that

you claim you don't want. You marry me and you'll never have to think about it again."

"That's very generous." She didn't bother to try to hide her smirk.

He smiled faintly, looking genuinely amused. "That's not how I meant it. I don't have any nefarious goals when it comes to Hollister's money."

"You don't have any nefarious goals *anymore*," she pointed out.

"True." He held up his hands as if he was calling for a truce. "All I meant was, if you don't want to think about the money, you don't want to obsess about the money, then marrying a banker to do it for you seems like the perfect solution."

"Wow," she said dryly. "You sweet-talker. Way to sweep me off my feet."

"We're good together, Meg. I didn't think I needed to do a hard sell to convince you of that. I think we'll be good together as a family too."

"You realize you don't have to marry me to be a father to Pearl. You can be her father—a real father to her—without us being married. Lots of men do it."

"I know that." He stood, shoving his hand through his hair. "But that's not what I want. I want to be a full-time father to her. I want us all together. After last night, I was hoping you wanted that too."

Of course, that was what he would think. Why wouldn't he?

He certainly wouldn't be the first man who tried to wrangle things so that he got exactly what he wanted with as little work as possible.

Sex between them was great. She couldn't deny that. It had been from the start. So why should he settle for being a long-distance father if he could talk her into marrying him? It would be a lot less work for him all around. And as a bonus, he could earn that redemption that he hadn't even realized he wanted.

She glanced up to find him watching her, subtle signs of his frustration showing in the tilt of his shoulders and his pinched lips.

Since he was clearly waiting for an answer, she shrugged. "I just don't know."

"What is it you want me to say?" he asked. "You want me to beg? You want the big romantic gesture? You want me down on one knee swearing my eternal devotion?"

She looked away, letting out a laugh that sounded more bitter than amused.

Yes. She did want all that. Of course she did. Every cynical, jeering word he said made her pulse pound, because that was exactly what she wanted. She didn't want a marriage because it was convenient. She didn't want to marry him just so she never had to think about money again. She wanted to marry him because he begged her to do it. Because he couldn't live without her. Because he needed her.

The fact that she wanted all those things scared the hell out of her.

She didn't think of herself as a terribly romantic person. She was practical and reasonable and logical. Except when it came to Grant.

When it came to Grant, she wanted it all.

Probably because she was already giving it all. She was already all in. At some point in the past few weeks, she'd not only forgiven Grant for breaking her heart the first time, she'd foolishly given it to him again. And he was too damn dense to realize it.

He was watching her. Waiting. Expectant.

He arched an eyebrow and gave her a smile that sent the butterflies in her stomach fluttering. "What do you say? Will you marry me?"

But before she could answer, Laney pushed open the door and walked into the courtyard. "Pearl is out of surgery. The doctor is waiting to talk to you."

Sixteen

Nothing was capable of mashing a man's ego like asking a woman for her hand in marriage and getting no real response.

But maybe that was his fault for asking while Pearl was still in surgery. Maybe it was a lame move to ask while Meg was emotionally vulnerable and exhausted. And, yeah, he probably should have worked a little harder on the presentation. But he'd poured his heart out to her, both last night and today. It should have been enough. And, yeah, the timing was crap. But sitting there in that serenity garden, waiting to hear how Pearl's surgery had gone, staring into that fountain, he'd been absolutely certain of one thing: no matter what happened with Pearl, he didn't want to lose Meg.

Yet here they were, nearly two hours after talking with the surgeon and the anesthesiologist, after having spent a full hour sitting by Pearl's side waiting for her to wake up, and Meg still hadn't said a word.

In fact, she'd barely looked at him. She'd hugged him, clung to him, cried with relief in his arms, but she hadn't once looked him in the eye. Which was fine. Because Pearl was fine. Sweet precious Pearl had come through the surgery with flying colors. The hole in her heart would heal. After a few days in the hospital, she would come home.

He was thrilled and relieved. And beneath that, there was another more selfish relief. Now, he had more time.

Which it seemed he was really going to need.

Unfortunately, he'd never been good at waiting. So he paced the length of the tiny recovery room so many times the nurse finally told him he'd have to leave if he didn't stop.

The nurse had also told them that Pearl would be groggy for several hours. That she would drift in and out of sleep and that when she finally woke up she'd be confused.

All of which was true.

The whole time, Meg sat at Pearl's side, holding her hand and stroking it lightly and humming, tucking the blanket more tightly around her and only occasionally shifting position in her seat and stretching.

Pearl drifted in and out, the first time crying and scared, the second shivering and cold and scared, the third crying again, but the fourth time full-temper mad. And each time, Meg calmed her, gentle and soothing. When Pearl finally rose to wakefulness, she looked around the room, still confused, but finally looking more herself. When her eyes found Meg, she smiled. Then she turned her bright gaze to him and her smile broadened. She reached one chubby hand out to him. He took it in his own, his throat feeling unexpectedly tight as she smiled up at him.

Meg was wrong. He didn't want them because he thought it would redeem him. What he'd done to Meg... well, he could only hope that one day she'd forgive him. But redemption? He didn't need that anymore. He simply wasn't that guy. He just hoped Meg would realize that.

Pearl, still holding on to both their hands, brought her own hands together to clap them, as if she was choreographing a three-person game of patty-cake.

Still enchanted by Pearl, he wasn't even looking at Meg when she said, "Okay, I'll do it. I'll marry you."

When he turned to look at her, she wasn't looking at him either. That's when he figured it out. Maybe his proposal hadn't been that romantic, but her answer wasn't either.

Meg hadn't said yes because she loved him or because she needed him. She'd said yes because Pearl wanted them to be together.

If his proposal had been lame, then her acceptance was even lamer.

But screw it, he accepted it anyway. Because a yes for all the wrong reasons bought him much-needed time. He would find a way to win Meg's heart back.

It was nearly night by the time Pearl was moved out of post-op and into a room on the pediatric floor. Meg had stayed by her side the whole time she was in post-op, but when the nurse came to move her, Grant talked Meg into going down to the cafeteria to grab a bite to eat while he stayed with Pearl.

Part of her was afraid that Grant would want to talk about his proposal and her acceptance. Which she wasn't ready to do. She hardly knew herself why she'd said yes.

So, frankly, she was relieved when she walked through the waiting room on the way to the cafeteria and saw Dalton still there. He stood when she walked into the waiting room, as if he'd been waiting for her.

Walking toward him, she felt a deep flash of affection. He'd stayed here all day. This big brother she'd never known she wanted.

She smiled as he held out his arms to her. "You didn't have to stay," she said, resting her tired head against his chest.

He didn't say anything but just held her. More tightly than she expected. Almost as if he was taking comfort

as well as giving it. Then she slowly became aware that
the shirt under her cheek was pressed black broadcloth,
not the white knit cotton he'd had on earlier. She began
to lean back, and after another squeeze, he loosened his
grasp enough to let her. He kept his eyes tightly closed,
but she could see the lines of tension etched on his face.

Then he looked at her, his gaze heavy with grief. "Hollister died."

She sucked in a breath, even though she'd already
guessed the news.

"When?"

"This morning. While Pearl was in surgery. We all had
our phones off."

She glanced behind him to the sign on the wall that
read, Out of respect for the others waiting with you, please
silence your cell phones.

She looked up at Dalton, taking in the sorrow on his
face. Absorbing the way he still held tight to her. Wondering how great his grief must be.

It was so hard for her. So confusing.

She had known of Hollister her whole life. He wasn't
just her father. He was the bogeyman hiding in the closet.
The monster who could come take her away if he wanted.
The Darth Vader to her living-in-hiding Princess Leia. Her
feelings for him were complicated but rarely conflicted.

But Dalton's? Dalton's relationship with Hollister—all
of her brothers', for that matter—must be so much more
layered than her own. She didn't even know how to comfort them, no matter how she might want to.

"I'm so sorry," she murmured over and over again.

When Dalton finally pulled away, he said, "There's
something else I need to talk to you about."

"Okay. Anything." But how could she handle anything
else? This day had been too much. From Pearl's surgery to
Grant's proposal to this. How could she bear anything more?

"Laney told me she overheard Grant proposing to you."

Unsure what to say to that, Meg simply nodded.

"I'm not going to tell you not to marry him." Dalton turned away from her slightly, running a hand through his already rumpled hair. "Jesus, I don't know what to think about Grant anymore. But Hollister's death. The changes in his will. It complicates things."

"I know." Even though she'd been trying not to think about the money—all that money that she didn't even want. That she'd never wanted.

"No. You don't know. There are things about Grant that I haven't told you. And I'm pretty sure he hasn't either."

Seventeen

Of all people, Grant should have enjoyed the cosmic justice surrounding Hollister's death. The man had died alone while his entire family had been off nurturing the granddaughter he'd never even met. It was a fittingly anticlimactic end for such a selfish, manipulative bastard. He'd spent his whole life trying to make his family dance to his tune, but in the end, none of them had.

Grant should have appreciated it and maybe he would have if Meg hadn't seemed so distraught over her father's death.

Grant tried to think his way around it because as he saw it, she had nothing to mourn. Still, the day of Hollister's death had been a hard one on Meg. The stress and relief of Pearl's surgery, followed by Hollister's death. It was a lot. Enough to break anyone.

And the days following it were no better. Meg was constantly at the hospital, except when she was with the Cains. Yes, all the work of Hollister's funeral had been handled ahead of time and no one expected her to make any decisions, but she still insisted on attending the viewing. The day of the funeral itself, her friend Janine came the entire day to sit with Pearl in hospital.

The whole time, Meg seemed oddly disconnected. Not

only from her grief, but also from Grant. She wouldn't touch him, barely talked to him and seemed unable to even look in him in the eye.

He told himself over and over that everyone grieved differently. That in a relationship so new she might not be comfortable yet opening up to him that way. But he still didn't like it and he simply couldn't shake the feeling something was deeply wrong.

A fear which was confirmed when he came home one day to find Meg packing up the last of her belongings. Pearl would still be in the hospital for a few more days. But all her toys and Pack 'N Play were already shoved into the back of Meg's Chevy, which didn't bode well.

And, damn it, Meg still wasn't looking at him.

He stopped in the doorway to the bedroom, blocking her way. "Are you going to tell me what's wrong or were you just going to disappear?"

"The way you did when you left me?"

"Touché." But when she stopped in front of him, suit-case in hand, he didn't step aside. Instead, he nudged her chin up so she'd meet his gaze. He didn't like the simmer-ing resentment he saw there.

"Why didn't you tell me you owned nearly twenty per-cent of Cain Enterprises?"

Shock flashed through him, but he recovered quickly. "It's actually only—"

"Why didn't you tell me that you've been buying up stock of my father's company?"

Regret crashed through him. He'd known this day was coming. Some part of him had known, even though he'd pushed it aside and buried it deep. Even though he'd told himself that she wouldn't care because she hated Hollis-ter almost as much as he did. Maybe more. She certainly had more reason to hate Hollister.

Maybe he should have protested. Maybe he would have

if he didn't think her anger was justified. And maybe if it had been only anger in her expression, he would have. It wasn't her anger that crushed him, it was her anguish.

"What?" she demanded. "You're not going to offer up some excuse? You're not going to protest that the subject just didn't come up? That in the past month that I've lived in your house, it never crossed your mind?"

"No. I'm not."

"Because it seems to me that it should have come up."

"Yes. It should have."

This only angered her more. "Would you stop being so damn reasonable!"

"What is it you want me to be? What do you want me to say?"

"I just want confirmation. Just to be perfectly clear, two and a half years ago, you found me and seduced me. And I finally get it. It wasn't just revenge against Hollister. You wanted the stock you thought would eventually come to me. But then you changed your mind. Or maybe you figured out that Hollister had no idea I existed and I wasn't going to get the stock. Whatever the reason, you cut bait and left."

"I left because I realized I was falling in love with you." For the first time, he said the words aloud. For the first time, he admitted it to himself.

But she ignored him. "So you came back here and started buying up all the Cain Enterprises stock you could get your hands on."

He reached for her, desperate for her to hear him. "If we're being clear, then listen to me. I left because I was falling in love with you. I left because I didn't want to hurt you."

"As recently as a month ago, you were still buying up Cain Enterprises stock. Do you deny it?"

"Of course I don't deny it. Why would I deny something you could easily prove?"

"Then you admit that you're still scheming to take over Cain Enterprises?"

"No, I don't admit that at all. A month ago, yes. But not now."

"Why?" she demanded. "Why not now? Because you don't have to scheme anymore? All you have to do is wait?"

"No. I'm not scheming anymore—to use your word— because I don't care about Cain Enterprises. I care—"

"Right." She didn't give him a chance to finish. She couldn't bear to hear it. "All your life you've been angling to take down Cain Enterprises, except now you suddenly don't give a rat's ass about it. That's mighty convenient."

"No. That's love. You want to know why I don't want to take down Cain Enterprises anymore? It's because I realized I love you. And when I realized that, taking down Cain Enterprises suddenly seemed like a pretty stupid idea."

For a long moment she just stared at him. Then, instead of the smile he expected, or the joy, or even the confusion—hell, that he could have done something with—instead of any of that, anger spread slowly over her face.

"Oh, so you love me now?"

"Yes."

"That's so…" She was shaking her head. "Convenient," she repeated with disgust.

He nearly laughed. "Trust me, loving you has been the least convenient thing I've ever done."

Confusion flickered across her face, momentarily obscuring the anger and rage, but then she pushed it away, physically slashing out her hand. "If we get married, my Cain Enterprises stock combined with yours suddenly means you have enough to take over the company. Not by a lot, but enough. You and I together would have more than Dalton, Cooper and Griffin combined."

"You think I care about that? I don't." The words surprised him, even as they were coming out of his mouth, because until this moment, he hadn't realized they were true.

"I think hurting Hollister is all you've ever cared about."

And until he'd met Meg, that had been true. All the work he'd done to make Sheppard Bank and Trust a success, he'd done to prove Hollister wrong—to prove that the banking crumbs Hollister had left his father could be worth more. He'd done it because it meant more leverage to bring down Hollister. He'd worked his whole life to take down Cain Enterprises and now it meant nothing to him.

"What are you saying?" he asked. "That you don't want to marry me unless I sign some sort of prenup that protects your shares of Cain Enterprises?"

She blinked, looking surprised. Her voice sounded as dazed as she suddenly looked. "That's what Dalton suggested."

"Fine. I'll sign whatever prenup you want. I'll sign whatever prenup the Cains want."

And he realized he meant it. And he realized what it meant. He would put himself completely at their mercy.

The Cains—whom he had hated and distrusted all his life. He would put himself at their mercy. Gladly. Because the idea of losing everything wasn't as scary as the idea of losing Meg.

"You just don't get it," she said, sounding numb. "If I feel like I need a prenup, that means I don't trust you. And I don't think I can ever trust you. I can't marry someone I can't trust."

Her declaration knocked him back on his heels. "You're saying you can't marry me. Because of Cain Enterprises. Because Dalton said you can't trust me."

She met his gaze finally. "I'm saying I can't marry you

because I don't trust you. I'm saying after what you did when we first met, I'll never be able to trust you."

"I offered to sign a prenup," he said tightly.

"I don't want a prenup. I want a husband who I believe when he says he loves me."

And that's what it came down to. He'd bared his heart and she didn't believe him. He'd practically groveled and she didn't care.

"Do you have any idea what I've offered you?" he snapped.

She blinked, as if surprised by the anger in his voice. As if she honestly hadn't seen it coming. Then she pressed her lips together. "Yeah. You offered me money. The only thing you actually care about."

She turned then as if to walk out. As if she could just walk away from him. From the life together he'd been planning.

Before she reached the door, he said, "You're acting like a child." She paused, slowly turning around to face him. She might have looked sad. Shocked. Hurt. He couldn't see it past his own anger. "Wanting to trust someone so much you don't need a prenup? Do you realize how incredibly silly that sounds?"

"You're calling me a child?"

"I'm saying you're being naive. This is the world we live in. Prenups are a part of it. Not just for you and me. For everyone. It's not about trust or love or devotion. It's about common sense. You aren't some small-town baker anymore and you need to stop thinking like one. You're worth hundreds of millions of dollars. You're—"

"I don't want the money. I never wanted it."

"Too bad. You have it. Want it or not, it's yours. You're a woman with a lot of power now and you better start acting like it, because if you don't, people will be lining up to take advantage of you. And they will use anything they can to do it. They will use your emotions. They will use your kindness. They will use Pearl. And that's your mistake right there. Not that you don't trust me, but that you don't recognize that you won't ever be able to trust anyone again."

"That's not true," she said, looking shell-shocked. "There are plenty of people I trust."

"Right. Dalton, Griffin, Cooper. You trust them. Laney, Sydney, Portia. You opened right up to them. That kid in the hotel room next to yours. You practically treated him like family. Hell, you even warmed up to Gisele and I'm pretty sure she hasn't smiled since leaving Russia. You are willing to give second chances to everyone you meet. Except me. Fine. I'm done begging."

She took a step back, staggering until she caught hold of the doorknob behind her. Tears brimmed in eyes that couldn't even meet his gaze. She opened her mouth and his breath caught as he waited for her answer. But she didn't give one. Instead, she turned and fled. Taking everything that mattered to him with her.

Eighteen

Meg wasn't foolish enough to want Grant to come after her. No, she dreaded the very idea because she wasn't at all sure that she had the will to resist him if he did. Still, she was surprised when he didn't.

Grant Sheppard wasn't the sort of man who gave up easily. He wasn't the sort of man to walk away from a situation just because it got a little challenging.

In fact, she'd been so sure he would put up a fight, she'd preemptively asked her lawyer to finish up paperwork for joint custody. On her own, she couldn't have afforded a lawyer, not until Hollister's estate came out of probate—which, frankly, could be years from now. But Dalton, Griffin and Cooper had made good on their promise. They had provided enough money to tide her over so that she already felt—as Grant had promised—that she would never have to worry about money again.

The bills from the doctors and the hospital had not started arriving yet, but when they did, she would have no trouble paying them, though she had a sneaking suspicion Grant planned to just contact the billing department and take care of it before the bills ever got to her. Maybe she should act preemptively, but she couldn't yet work up the energy to care about pride when she was so emotionally battered.

Though, of course, she was thrilled about Pearl's recovery. Pearl had been released from the hospital the morning after Hollister's funeral. Grant had been there to help, but he'd refused to even meet Meg's gaze, and hadn't protested when she'd loaded Pearl into her own car and headed home to Victoria immediately. Something she appreciated, even though she'd pulled off the highway at the Dairy Queen in Bay City, where she'd gotten Pearl a Push-Up. And then she'd cried while she ate her own Dilly Bar.

By the time she'd driven into Victoria, she had it together. And after a few more days of recovery at home, Pearl seemed as good as new. The whole town enjoyed seeing her happily toddle around. And she delighted in showing off her scar to anyone who would look at it.

For Meg, recovery was slower. Frankly, it was exhausting being so happy about one thing and so miserable about another at the same time. She felt as though healing Pearl's heart had ripped a hole in her own.

How exactly was she supposed to keep this up? How was she supposed to recover from Grant a second time?

The first time had been hard enough. Only her pregnancy had snapped her out of it. From the moment she'd found out about Pearl, she'd simply been too busy to mope. She had no hope of another pregnancy. They'd used protection and she'd been on birth control. One unexpected, miracle pregnancy was more than any reasonable woman had a right to expect in life.

Instead, the best she could do was stay really busy. And bake. She could always bake.

So even though it was the middle of the afternoon on a Tuesday—the bakery's slowest time—and even though she had more than enough stock to get them through to the morning, Meg was busy in the kitchen, spooning sour cream into a measuring cup, trying to perfect her recipe for lemon-ginger cupcakes. She heard the bell ring over the door in the front of the shop and called out, "Janine, is that you?"

Janine, who had taken Pearl out for a walk a few minutes earlier, called out, "It's us!" A second later, Janine pushed through the swing door with one hip as she held Pearl on the other. "You should have seen our Pearl. There we were walking down Main Street and this helicopter flew overhead."

"That's strange," Meg said halfheartedly. Victoria was close enough to the Gulf of Mexico that a lot of people from Houston drove through it on the way to Port Lavaca or Port Aransas. The town got tourist traffic but not a lot of helicopters. "Any idea who it was?"

"Nope," Janine said as she set Pearl down on the counter opposite Meg. She held tight to Pearl so the little girl couldn't squirm off.

Pearl clapped her hands together. "Dada!"

Meg's heart broke a little. In the past month, Pearl had slowly been adding words to her vocabulary. Her newest language acquisition just killed Meg. Dada.

Pearl had been asking for Dada more and more lately. And Grant had never even heard her say it. Where the hell was he?

Forget the fact that Meg didn't want to see him. Pearl wanted to. And he'd sworn he wanted to be part of Pearl's life. So where was he?

And how dare he leave it to Meg to deal with Pearl's disappointed hopes on her own? To be fair, it didn't have to be this way. This was her doing. And she was prepared to cope with her own broken heart, but after their time together in Houston, Meg had been convinced that Grant was in Pearl's life to stay.

Meg wiped her hands off on her apron and came around

to pick up Pearl. Holding her daughter close, she murmured, "No, honey. It's not your daddy."

"Dada!" Pearl insisted.

"I know you miss him." Over Pearl's head, Meg caught Janine giving her a suspicious look and she turned away, burying her face in Pearl's hair to hide her expression. Because, yes, she missed Grant too. Damn it, what was wrong with her?

Before she could decide, her phone buzzed with a text. Annoyed, she fished it out of her back pocket, only to stare at it, confused.

"What's up, honey?" Janine asked. "You look worried."

"It's from Grant." She frowned, reading the text again. "He asked me and Pearl to meet him somewhere."

Janine propped her hand on her hip. "You haven't heard from that man in a month and now he sends you a text asking you to go to Houston to meet him. What a—"

"No. The address isn't in Houston. It's here in Victoria."

"Well, then, where does he want you to meet him?"

Meg clicked the link in the text and the map app opened up on her phone. She frowned, staring at that screen. "I think it's out by the old airfield."

Like most small towns in Texas, Victoria had a regional airport that was used mostly by crop dusters and the occasional recreational pilot. The address Grant had sent her was for a private hangar on the south side of the airport. Unlike many of the other hangars, this one seemed to have recently been given a fresh coat of paint. A sign above the open doors read Pearl Enterprises. There was a helicopter on the landing pad in front of the hangar. Pearl Enterprises was painted on the side of the helicopter as well.

The gate was open, so she drove in and parked in one of the available spots by the fence. As she unbuckled Pearl's car seat, Grant came out of the hangar. He was dressed in jeans and a gray Henley that made his shoulders look impossibly wide and his eyes look even grayer than usual.

She looked from him to the helicopter and back again. As soon as Pearl saw Grant, she started clapping her hands and squealing. She squirmed so much, eventually Meg had to set her down. Pearl broke out into a toddling run and barreled across the concrete toward Grant.

He scooped her up, twirling her around while Pearl squealed with delight.

"Dada, Dada, Dada!" she chanted.

At her words, Grant stilled, his expression frozen in a look of pure wonder. After a second, he smiled. "Wow, bean, you've got a word."

"Dada, Dada, Dada!" she said again, clearly thrilled he'd noticed.

Meg felt as if her heart was going to burst right out of her chest. Damn, they looked good together. Each of them so happy. So complete together.

He didn't look like a man capable of breaking Meg's heart. But he was. He had. And he would again every time she had to see him.

Mustering a little protective sarcasm, she said, "You bought our daughter a helicopter."

"No. Actually…" He paused to reach behind him and pulled something out of his back pocket. It was a sheath of triple-folded papers, which he handed out to her. "I bought *you* a helicopter."

"We didn't hear anything from you for a month. And now you show up here with a helicopter and I'm supposed to…what?" She glanced at the papers but didn't open them. Her protective coating was cracking. She wanted to throw something. To storm off. To slap him. To throw herself into his arms, the way Pearl had.

Before she could do any of those things, Grant closed the distance between them. He pulled her to him with his free arm. Pearl automatically threw her arms around Meg's neck. Grant pressed a kiss to her temple.

"Shh, it's all right."

"It's not all right!" God, she sounded as if she was crying. Was she crying?

"It's going to be all right," he murmured.

"You disappeared!" she accused. "For a month! We didn't hear anything from you and—"

"Missed me, did you?"

She punched at his arm weakly. "You can't ask a woman to marry you and then not contact her for a month. You can't say you want to be a part of a child's life and then not follow through."

"Fair enough. And it won't happen again."

"Damn straight it won't happen again!"

"But hear me out, okay?"

He was still holding her close. His lips were still near her temple, so every word was like a kiss. She forced herself to push away from him. She'd never be able to think straight with his lips against her skin.

"Okay," she said cautiously.

"When I proposed back at the hospital, I made a mistake. I didn't think it through."

Oh. Great. This was even better than she'd thought.

He must have seen the confusion on her face because he quickly continued, "I didn't have a plan. I thought that with Pearl's surgery out of the way, you'd go back to your life. You'd leave me. And I'd be screwed. So I proposed out of panic, with no real plan for how we would make it work. I didn't want to make the same mistake twice. So I waited until I believed I could convince you to give me another chance."

"Okay," she said again slowly. She glanced down at the folded papers. "What's this?"

"That's my plan. The highlights of it anyway." He

grinned, looking almost bashful. "There's an overview of the prenup I've had my lawyers working on. There's information about a trust I've put together for Pearl. You'll be the executor of the trust. It contains all my stock in Cain Enterprises. I can't break the trust. I'll never be able to touch that stock again. Which means, essentially, you're in charge of the biggest chunk of the company."

"But I don't—"

"I know you don't want that kind of control. I know it scares you. But ignoring it won't make it go away. Cain Enterprises is in your blood. It's who you are. And I know you don't want to leave Victoria or Sweet Things. That's who you are too. So that's what the helicopter is for. You don't have to be just a small-town baker or just a Houston socialite. You can be whatever you want."

"Grant, I—"

Now he reached for her again, taking her hand in his. "Look, I know you don't want the prenup. I know you want to be able to trust me without one, but I don't know how to make you trust me. I don't know how to convince you that I love you, other than to give you everything I have. The only way I know how to prove to you that I'm trustworthy is to trust you with my own heart. And then to hope you love me enough not to break it."

For a moment, she didn't know what to think or what to do.

Of course, she knew what she wanted. She wanted Grant. This incredible man who, somehow, inexplicably seemed to love her. She just wanted him. And she also wanted to believe in him. To believe in their love. But how could she do that?

"I don't know if I know how to trust you," she admitted.

"This prenup puts a lot of power in your hands. The trust for Pearl puts even more. I spent a lot of time and resources into acquiring that stock in Cain Enterprises. I'm essentially, putting the last few years of my life in your hands." He ducked his head, pressing a kiss to her temple and then to Pearl's. "I can't make you trust me. All I can do is prove that I trust you."

And somehow, that did it for her. He had devoted most of his life to taking down Cain Enterprises. And he was giving that up for her and Pearl. Between the stock in the trust and the stock owned by her and her brothers, there wasn't enough out there for him to ever again make a play for Cain Enterprises. He really had given up everything for her. "Look, I don't want to be with you because of Pearl," he continued. "And I don't want to be with you because you've made it easy for me." He gave a laugh that sounded equal parts amused and derisive. "Because God knows you haven't exactly made it easy. And I sure as hell don't want to be with you because of that stupid Cain Enterprises stock. I want to be with you because you're you. I want to be with you because when I'm with you, I can imagine being the kind of man I want to be. The kind of man my father would be proud of. The kind of man your grandfather would want for you."

When she looked around, there were signs of his love everywhere. The hangar he'd bought. The helicopter, which when she looked at it, had two logos painted beneath the Pearl Enterprises sign. One was the logo for Sheppard Bank and Trust. The other was the logo for Sweet Things.

And then she looked at Pearl, who was gazing lovingly up at Grant. Maybe she couldn't trust her own heart, but she could trust Pearl's. She did trust Pearl's heart.

All her life, Meg hadn't wanted to be like her mother. She hadn't wanted to be duped by a man. She hadn't wanted to be controlled by her heart. She hadn't wanted to have her heart broken and then never recover.

Well, maybe the way not to be her mother was to never fall in love.

Or maybe the way was simply to fall in love with a better guy.

Grant gave her hand a tug and she went into his arms.

Here he was. Her better guy.

"I thought you were done begging for second chances," she said.

"No. I just needed a new plan."

Her faith in him was so new, she almost couldn't put it into words, but she tried. "You wanted to know why I was so willing to trust everyone but you? It's because no one else has the power to hurt me like you do. I'm so happy to have brothers and sisters-in-law who care about Pearl and I, but none of them is as important to me as you are. Trusting you—" she began, but then corrected herself "—loving you is scary because I don't want to lose you again. But I want to try."

But he shook his head. "I don't want to just try to make this work. I want you to believe that it will work. I need you to know how much I love you."

All her doubts were gone. All that was left was hope and love and the belief that she was luckier than she'd ever dreamed of being.

Epilogue

Meg wasn't beside him when he woke up in the middle of the night. When he rolled over and realized she was gone, he reached for his phone to check the time. Midnight. The witching hour. Or, as it was known in their house, the baking hour.

He climbed out of bed, pulling on pajama bottoms as he made his way through the tiny bungalow to the kitchen. One of the first things he'd done after convincing Meg to marry him was buy back the bungalow she'd grown up in. He'd paid twice what she'd gotten for it, but it was worth it. The house felt like a part of her. A part of their history. It was the house he'd first fallen in love with her in. There were hard memories there too, but he was determined to make her so happy, the good outweighed the bad.

Hopefully today, their wedding day, would count among the good memories.

He found Meg right where he knew he would: in the kitchen, humming along to some song only she heard while she stirred something on the stove.

He stepped up behind her, slipping his arm around her waist and pulling her back against him. She sighed as she settled into his arms.

"You didn't have to get up," she murmured.

He cupped her breast, nearly groaning when she arched her back slightly, rubbing her bottom against his erection. "You don't think I'd get out of bed for this?"

She twisted just enough to plant a kiss on his jaw.

He had to fight the temptation to turn her around, to lift her onto the counter and take her right there. But she was whisking what looked like chocolate pudding and he knew from experience how quickly it would scald.

Unlike most brides-to-be, Meg had spent the past few days baking up a storm. The fridge at the pie shop already contained a wedding cake and a bridegroom's cake. Neither was big, since the ceremony here in Victoria wouldn't be nearly as large as the reception they'd have next week in Houston. The ceremony today would be mostly family and close friends.

Together their families made a strangely cohesive unit. Three and half years ago, he would never have believed how comfortable he now felt around the Cains. He never would have imagined that he could sip a beer in Dalton's backyard while barbecue cooked on the grill, or that he and Griffin would meet for coffee to discuss business trends. That he would spend Christmas up at Cooper's gorgeous home in the mountains of Utah. Now, after a yearlong engagement to Meg, all of those things seemed natural.

Of course, he also never would have imagined that his favorite TV show would involve talking time-traveling dinosaurs. Which just proved that sometimes the unexpected were the best parts of life.

He reached a hand around Meg to swipe a finger through the warm pudding. "Are you making another s'more pie?"

She swatted playfully at his hand before he got the pudding into his mouth.

"It's Pearl's favorite," Meg said with a little smile.

"It's mine too," he admitted, savoring the heat from

peppers and the way they complemented the smokiness of the dark chocolate.

She stopped stirring long enough to look over her shoulder. "You never told me that."

Tipping up her chin, he pressed a kiss to her full lips. "You make a lot of amazing food, but the first time you made this was the day I realized I loved you. Of course it's my favorite."

He'd been stupid. He'd nearly blown it. He'd wasted too much time, but in the end he'd won her back. So yeah, this pie, with its heat, its many layers, its simplicity and its complications, it was his favorite.

* * * * *

*If you loved the lost heiress's romance,
pick up the other books in the*
AT CAIN'S COMMAND *series*

*ALL HE EVER WANTED
ALL HE REALLY NEEDS
A BRIDE FOR THE BLACK SHEEP BROTHER*

Available now from Harlequin Desire!

*If you're on Twitter, tell us what you think of
Harlequin Desire! #harlequindesire*

COMING NEXT MONTH FROM

HARLEQUIN®

Desire

Available June 2, 2015

#2377 WHAT THE PRINCE WANTS
Billionaires and Babies • by Jules Bennett
Needing time to heal, a widowed prince goes incognito. He hires a
live-in nanny for his infant daughter but soon finds he wants the woman
for *himself*. Is he willing to cross the line from professional to personal?

#2378 CARRYING A KING'S CHILD
Dynasties: The Montoros • by Katherine Garbera
Torn between running his family's billion-dollar shipping business
and assuming his ancestral throne, Rafe Montoro needs to let off
some steam. But his night with a bartending beauty could change
everything—because now there's a baby on the way...

#2379 PURSUED BY THE RICH RANCHER
Diamonds in the Rough • by Catherine Mann
Driven by his grandmother's dying wish, a Texas rancher must choose
between his legacy and the sexy single mother who unknowingly holds
the fate of his heart—and his inheritance—in her hands.

#2380 THE SHEIKH'S SECRET HEIR
by Kristi Gold
Billionaire Tarek Azzmar knows a secret that will destroy the royal family
who shunned him. But the tables turn when he learns his lover is near
and dear to the royal family *and* she's pregnant with his child.

#2381 THE WIFE HE COULDN'T FORGET
by Yvonne Lindsay
Olivia Jackson steals a second chance with her estranged husband
when he loses his memories of the past two years. But when he finally
remembers *everything*, will their reconciliation stand the ultimate test?

#2382 SEDUCED BY THE CEO
Chicago Sons • by Barbara Dunlop
When businessman Riley Ellis learns that his rival's wife has a secret
twin sister, he seduces the beauty as leverage and then hires her to
keep her close. But now he's trapped by his own lies...and his desires...

**YOU CAN FIND MORE INFORMATION ON UPCOMING HARLEQUIN® TITLES,
FREE EXCERPTS AND MORE AT WWW.HARLEQUIN.COM.**

HDCNM0515

REQUEST YOUR FREE BOOKS!
2 FREE NOVELS PLUS 2 FREE GIFTS!

HARLEQUIN®

Desire

ALWAYS POWERFUL, PASSIONATE AND PROVOCATIVE

YES! Please send me 2 FREE Harlequin® Desire novels and my 2 FREE gifts (gifts are worth about $10). After receiving them, if I don't wish to receive any more books, I can return the shipping statement marked "cancel." If I don't cancel, I will receive 6 brand-new novels every month and be billed just $4.55 per book in the U.S. or $5.24 per book in Canada. That's a savings of at least 13% off the cover price! It's quite a bargain! Shipping and handling is just 50¢ per book in the U.S. and 75¢ per book in Canada.* I understand that accepting the 2 free books and gifts places me under no obligation to buy anything. I can always return a shipment and cancel at any time. Even if I never buy another book, the two free books and gifts are mine to keep forever.

225/326 HDN GH2P

Name _____ (PLEASE PRINT) _____

Address _____ Apt. # _____

City _____ State/Prov. _____ Zip/Postal Code _____

Signature (if under 18, a parent or guardian must sign)

Mail to the **Reader Service:**
IN U.S.A.: P.O. Box 1867, Buffalo, NY 14240-1867
IN CANADA: P.O. Box 609, Fort Erie, Ontario L2A 5X3

Want to try two free books from another line?
Call 1-800-873-8635 or visit www.ReaderService.com.

* Terms and prices subject to change without notice. Prices do not include applicable taxes. Sales tax applicable in N.Y. Canadian residents will be charged applicable taxes. Offer not valid in Quebec. This offer is limited to one order per household. Not valid for current subscribers to Harlequin Desire books. All orders subject to credit approval. Credit or debit balances in a customer's account(s) may be offset by any other outstanding balance owed by or to the customer. Please allow 4 to 6 weeks for delivery. Offer available while quantities last.

Your Privacy—The Reader Service is committed to protecting your privacy. Our Privacy Policy is available online at www.ReaderService.com or upon request from the Reader Service.

We make a portion of our mailing list available to reputable third parties that offer products we believe may interest you. If you prefer that we not exchange your name with third parties, or if you wish to clarify or modify your communication preferences, please visit us at www.ReaderService.com/consumerchoice or write to us at Reader Service Preference Service, P.O. Box 9062, Buffalo, NY 14240-9062. Include your complete name and address.

SPECIAL EXCERPT FROM

HARLEQUIN®

Desire

*Will Rafe Montoro have to choose between the throne
and newfound fatherhood?*

*Read on for a sneak preview of
CARRYING A KING'S CHILD,
a DYNASTIES: THE MONTOROS novel
by USA TODAY bestselling author
Katherine Garbera.*

Pregnant!

He knew Emily wouldn't be standing in his penthouse apartment telling him this if he wasn't the father. His first reaction was joy.

A child.

It wasn't something he'd ever thought he wanted, but the idea that Emily was carrying his baby seemed right to him.

Maybe that was just because it gave him something other than his royal duties to think about. He'd been dreading his trip to Alma. He was flattered that the country that had once driven his family out had come back to them, asked them—him, as it turned out—to be the next king. But he had grown up here in Miami. He didn't want to be a stuffy royal.

He didn't want European paparazzi following him around and trying to catch him doing anything that would bring shame to his family. Including having a child out of wedlock.

"Rafe, did you hear what I said?"

"Yeah, I did. Are you sure?" he asked at last.

She gave him a fiery look from those aqua-blue eyes of hers. He'd seen the passionate side of her nature, and he guessed he was about to witness her temper. Hurricane Em was about to unleash all of her fury on him, and he didn't blame her one bit.

He held his hand up. "Slow down, Red. I didn't mean are you sure it's mine. I meant…are you sure you're pregnant?"

"Damned straight. And I wouldn't be here if I wasn't sure it was yours. Listen, I don't want anything from you. I know you can't turn your back on your family and marry me, and frankly, we only had one weekend together, so I'd have to say no to a proposal anyway. But…I don't want this kid to grow up without knowing you."

"Me neither."

She glanced up, surprised.

He'd sort of surprised himself. But it didn't seem right for a kid of his to grow up without him. He wanted that. He wanted a chance to impart the Montoro legacy…not the one newly sprung on him involving a throne, but the one he'd carved for himself in business. "Don't look shocked."

"You've kind of got a lot going on right now. And having a kid with me isn't going to go over well."

"Tough," he said. "I still make my own decisions."

Available June 2015 wherever
Harlequin® Desire books and ebooks are sold.

www.Harlequin.com

THE WORLD IS BETTER WITH

Romance

Harlequin has everything from contemporary, passionate and heartwarming to suspenseful and inspirational stories.

Whatever your mood,
we have a romance just for you!

Connect with us to find your next great read, special offers and more.

f /HarlequinBooks

🐦 @HarlequinBooks

www.HarlequinBlog.com

www.Harlequin.com/Newsletters

A *Romance* FOR EVERY MOOD™

www.Harlequin.com

Desire burns deepest after dark...

WHATEVER YOU LIKE

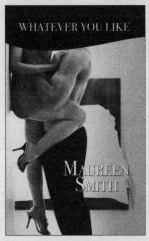

MAUREEN SMITH

By day, Lena Morrison is an ambitious grant writer. By night, she's an escort to some of Chicago's most successful men. Sex isn't on the menu—just companionship and sparkling conversation. But when tycoon Roderick Brand hires Lena, their electric attraction leads to an attractive proposal that Lena can't resist. Can she keep business and pleasure separate? Does she even want to?

"Smith does a masterful job...so intriguing the story is hard to put down!"—*RT Book Reviews* on *TOUCH OF HEAVEN*

Coming the first week of November 2010 wherever books are sold.

REQUEST YOUR FREE BOOKS!

2 FREE NOVELS
PLUS 2 FREE GIFTS!